TALES OF DORIAS

Book 1: Kahlen's Burden

Paul H. LeSage

DORRANCE
PUBLISHING CO
EST. 1920
PITTSBURGH, PENNSYLVANIA 15238

Dorrance Publishing
585 Alpha Drive, Suite 103
Pittsburgh, PA 15238
Visit our website at www.dorrancepublishing.com

ISBN: 978-1-4809-3638-6
eISBN: 978-1-4809-3661-4

1.

As dusk encroached upon the two armies, slivers of sunlight danced off of his warrior's armor to the enemy's blades. From the safety of the war tent, King Corning could almost imagine his nine year old self trying to catch the flash bugs that followed the great herd of oxen grazing lazily on the lush, dense grasses of the Range. Of course, instead of the low grunts and snorts from his hoofed, childhood companions, the shrill screams from the dying and the mournful wails of the wounded kept him in the present. With a sigh of resigned acceptance, the King turned his attention to the courier who stood wide-eyed, clutching his horse's reigns in his left hand and holding his right hand in a fist, pressed to the center of his chest, in Tantra's traditional salute.

The King made a simple motion of his hand for the courier to approach, and sensing the courier's wariness, arched his right eyebrow inquisitively, pursed his lips and with a touch of exasperation asked "well?" The courier cleared his throat, "My liege, I bring news from the front." The King was never a patient man and he glared at the courier. King Corning's self-proclaimed gift was in balancing the needs of his country with the needs of the aristocracy. With a hint of menacing, the King mocked his courier. "News from the front? We are living in the bloody front. Unless you are here to tell me that those two lawless bastards have relented and are ready to surrender then you'll be leading the next wave to the field." The courier glanced toward the battlefield and back to his King. "My liege, I bring word from your trappers." The courier, finding his nerve, spoke more calmly. "The trappers had been tracking game, and less than ten miles beyond the ridge they came upon a large host." The King took a moment to gather his thoughts and called for his spy glass. He asked the courier, "Is it Wintersbane reserves? Or, could it be Governor Sorling and his suspiciously absent forces?" King Corning trained his view to the ridge, an elevation of no more than thirty feet above the battlefield but angled slightly downward, and at the moment there was no sign of the mysterious host.

"Doubtful, Sire," replied the courier. The courier then added, "They were apparently singing in a strange tongue and made no attempt to confront the trappers." King Corning absentmindedly tapped the spyglass against his lips, exhaled slowly and turned back to the courier. As he placed his right hand on the courier's shoulder, the courier reflexively knelt and bowed his head. The King nodded his approval and squeezed the courier's shoulder, prompting an expectant look. The King then called for his war council. As men hurried to respond, the King exclaimed, "Make sure this man," he said, pointing to the courier, "is well fed and provided a fresh horse so he can go and find that coward Sorling." As the King entered the war tent, he could be heard commanding one of his generals. "Sound the recall. We can finish killing each other in daylight".

· · ·

"Where is my wench?" Bellowed Prince Oren, twin brother of Mallon, the two oldest sons of the late King Ottrun. Heirs to the throne of Wintersbane, they have spent more time proving their prowess in the leisure houses of Castleton than in the field drawing blood. A flirty, throaty and well-practiced "here my Prince" floated from behind the tent flap barely concealing the auburn haired camp follower calling herself Autumn. She added "and I've somehow lost my clothes". Oren grinned, grabbed a mug of ale from a soldier walking by, drank it down and playfully chased the camp follower inside his tent. Struggling out of his armor, Oren pleaded, "get over here woman, I'm to relieve my brother soon and I need you to relieve me first."

Oren wasted no time in putting the camp follower's skills to the test, and while recharging with more ale the sounds of Tantra's horns blared. Oren poked his head out of the tent and called to one of his personal guards. "What the hell is that racket, Timbor?" The guardsman replied in deadpan fashion. "I believe King Cornball is calling his children to supper." Oren laughed the hearty laugh of a man who had never faced death. The kind of laugh that follows the bawdy tavern tales men tell when trying to impress each other. The kind of laugh that men lose when they've tripped over the entrails of their fellow soldiers one too many times. The kind of laugh reserved for children and cowards.

Oren had just finished a second go with Autumn when a new, haggard sounding horn belched the approach of a rider. With the skies darkening so quickly, troops returning from the field, bitched at the lack of fires, and crowded around the first few to be lit barking for food and drink or for the comfort of a cold tent and a warm woman. The rider dismounted and weaved among the troops until he approached Prince Oren's tent where Timbor blocked his way. Timbor sized up the rider. "Whaddya want?" The rider—a grizzled, weather beaten man with small eyes, removed his hood and calmly explained, "I am Prince Mallon's long scout, Hark. I was tasked with finding any reinforcements heading to Corning's camp." From inside the tent, giggles and grunts and the occasional "yes, my Prince," began in earnest. Timbor stepped away from the tent entrance and closed the distance between he and Hark. "So, as you can tell, Prince Mallon isn't here yet and Prince Oren, he's busy." Hark glanced downward, clenched his teeth and continued. "You may want to tell the Prince to hurry it up a bit." Timbor's incredulous look turned to bemusement as he said "it's your funeral" and announced to his Prince that he was entering the tent.

A not so muffled exclamation of displeasure pierced the tent flap a moment before Oren—head tilted in what could only be described as utter bewilderment, rushed toward Hark. "This better be fucking good," Oren ranted. As Hark was about to speak, Autumn, burst through the tent flap, not a care in the world nor a scrap of clothing on her body. "My Prince," she said. "Will you be putting the horse back in the stable?" Oren held his finger to his lips quieting Autumn for a moment. Nodding at Timbor and then at Hark, "Timbor, if this rider reports good news send this woman to his tent when I'm done with her." Timbor raised both eyebrows and smirked while asking, "And what happens to him if it's bad news?" Oren, eyes gleaming and a devilish grin upon his face said, "Well, Timbor, if its bad news, he still gets the girl...but then he has to marry her."

Prince Mallon, sweaty and dirty yet strangely free of blood could be heard several tents down exclaiming to anyone who would listen how "those Tantra goat lovers retreated not because of the darkness, but due to the sword in my hand that would pierce their men or the sword in my pants that would pierce their women." The tired, murmured chortle belied the knowledge that as the men saw it; their great Prince was great at racing at the back of the lines and acting like he was charging with his troops only to pull up just before tasting steel. Of course, when the horn sounded and the men from Tantra eased back defensively, the Prince could have, should have, pressed forward and taken advantage of the moment and crushed them. Instead, the Prince saw the opportunity to ride to the front and mock his foes pretending as if he'd been in the muck all day and leading a rousing victory speech. Then, Mallon's thought turned to wine and women.

"Oren? Where are you my brother?" called Mallon. Oren looked to Timbor and said, "You'd better go get him, he may want to hear what Hark here is desperate to tell me." Mallon shook his head and interrupted Hark. "Wait, again. Say it again so that I can sort this out." Hark, steadfast and showing no sign of the growing impatience that welled within, repeated his report albeit a bit more simply than before. "My Prince, while I was returning from the ruins where two thousand men traveling under Sorling's banner made camp, I happened upon a small group of scouts and trappers that were making their way several miles south of the battlefield. I was worried that Tantra was committing more forces in an attempt to outflank us." Mallon, face obscured by the chalice of wine he as greedily sucking down, gurgled, "out with it, do we have an army sniffing up our skirts from behind or not?" "No, my Prince," issued Hark. "If I may, my Prince, what I found was something that neither I nor the scouts from Tantra expected. At first, I thought with the way those scouts hurried away that it may have been those stubborn sots from Blackstone leaving the New Road to get in on the glory but instead, it was a host so vast and foreign that I could not identify them."

Mallon wiped wine from his mouth and walked over to Oren. "Brother" spoke Mallon "what do you think of all this?" Oren grinned, "I think, dear brother, that Hark is about to become a married man."

2.

When he was a small boy, Kahlen would often pretend that he was a knight in service to his Queen. He would always introduce himself to the clammers and fishermen as Sir Kahlen of House Bowsprit. The majority of the time he was met with tussled hair and a welcome laugh by the hearty souls who called Crescent Bay home. The Bay, nestled in the northeastern most coastline of Tantra and lapped by the edge of the Green Sea, was a mirror of the old ways. The village seldom saw outsiders travel in through the Northern Trail and even fewer ships dared the northern trip up from East Watch as Tantra's fleet in the Green Sea, known as Cutters, were built to hug the coastline moving southward toward the Wintersbane border while utilizing the strong current. The Cutters were agile ships. They held no more than twenty men; the majority was crossbowmen and was shallow in the keel. The first time those ships set sail the men on shore marveled at how the ships sliced through the chop and thus the Cutters were born.

Today, the village of Crescent Bay was preparing a feast the likes of which had not been seen in three hundred years. The men had come in early from the sea and the nets were coiled neatly to the side of the dock. The boats bobbed absentmindedly tied to their moorings. There was an expectant murmur, at first like a dull buzz from a distant fly but as the sun set it grew louder until the unmistakable sounds of a party could be heard for miles. Music, food, wine, ale, and more food spilled out of Dock master Averill's home. So too did Kahlen and his intended, Danielle. They held hands and walked slowly down the grass path toward the harbor steps. The celebration continued and the occasional hoot or cheer echoed around the two as they watched the first sliver of the moon creep above the water. A few hundred yards into the Bay sat a stumpy grass and moss covered island, known as Bay Heart, where an ancient marble altar and fire pit were barely silhouettes. Danielle spoke first, "Kahlen, everything this night is in your honor. Your name." Kahlen glanced back over his shoulder toward the sounds of the party and said wistfully, "I can't believe it. The whole town is at your father's house. I'd heard that the last man to receive 'no blessing' was found dead less than a mile from the village."

"Kahlen," Danielle spoke softly, "this is your last night do you want to spend it talking of men hundreds of years gone or with me?" Kahlen turned with a barely audible "huh?" His eyes widened as Danielle slid her gown over her shoulders and rocked it off of her waist. The lithe, taught skinned beauty stood naked before him and beckoned him forward. Kahlen stumbled while rising to his feet and as he righted himself, he watched Danielle slip easily into the water and head for the Bay Heart. Kahlen, hands on his hips called out, "Really? A swim on my last night?" Danielle turned to her back, arching her body so that Kahlen could make out all of the parts that made her the most desirable woman in the Bay. Before turning over to continue her swim, she teased, "C'mon I've got a surprise for you." Kahlen began stepping into the water but before he took a second step Danielle pouted. "That's not fair, I have no clothes on". Kahlen, feeling the blush that only the naive experience when something so obvious is explained to them, disrobed and started to swim.

Kahlen could not remember the last time he'd swum to the Heart. He knew that watching Danielle on the beach and in the water was a memory that he'd take to his grave. Kahlen reached the stony outcropping of the Heart and scaled the path worn from the men of the First World thousands of years before. Dripping with salt water and anticipation, Kahlen stood under the broken remnant of what was likely a church or shrine and stared at Danielle who stood behind the growing fire she had started moments earlier. Kahlen thought how the fire was burning so strongly. Too strongly for a fire so freshly set. "How did you get that fire going so quickly?" he asked. Danielle laughed and moved a step closer to the flames. Kahlen's thoughts of the fire were doused as Danielle began moving her hands over her body. "Kahlen, my love," she beckoned. "I have two presents for you. The second is one that I will give you. The first is one I want you to take." With that, Danielle laid herself upon the altar and held her arms outstretched, begging Kahlen forward.

Kahlen laid his head upon Danielle's breast. They were both breathing raggedly, their hearts beating rapidly; they did not need to speak. Those moments could never be duplicated. For the first time they were one. As Danielle stepped from the altar, Kahlen watched. He watched not as the shy boy who first threw a handful of chum at the red headed chatterbox that followed him from boat to cart ten years ago. No, he watched as only a man who has known love can watch. He watched, he feared, as a man who will never know this love again. Danielle was moving a large stone that was resting against a shattered pillar. Kahlen sat up, as the flames from the pit framed Danielle's body. It looked like the flames were licking at her and his passion rose once more. Kahlen eased from the altar and before Danielle could speak placed his mouth upon hers and decided that her second gift would have to wait. He wasn't finished with her first gift just yet.

They laid there, staring at the full moon as it gazed down upon them. Danielle kissed Kahlen's neck and chest then eased up from the ground and over to the rock to recover whatever she had hidden. Danielle returned with a thickly woven sack. Danielle knelt beside Kahlen and with a hint of sadness began pulling items from the sack. "These are for you," she started. She pulled out a pair of padded, thick leather pants and the softest long sleeved shirt he'd ever felt. "Kahlen, we have all been preparing for this day. Widow Harper traded two carts full of dried fish to the cloth merchant visiting North Watch a few months ago. That's why she's been having you try on her husband's old clothes to be sure of the right fit." Kahlen was resting upon one elbow and peeking at the shirt in Danielle's hand. These shoes are called stompers and when my father had to personally deliver an order to the guards at East Watch he saw them and knew that you would need them. He accepted the boots as payment instead of money." Kahlen scratched his forehead and Danielle knew that he was putting it all together. "This last item is from me," and with that she held out a long curved hunting knife. Kahlen lifted the knife from Danielle's hands and stood. He stepped closer to the fire to better appreciate what he was holding. The blade looked sturdy and very sharp. It was polished metal nearly a foot long. The handle was a pale iridescent stone. He could barely make out the carving. Danielle cleared her throat "the handle is made from a piece of the altar stone. It took me months to fashion it all together. It took almost as long to inscribe it." Kahlen felt the ridges but could not make out the inscription. "It says," Danielle paused, "The Knight of Crescent Bay".

Kahlen took a deep breath and noticed how far west the moon had travelled. "I think" he offered, "we should make our way back home." A small crack of despair deflated the moment and spurred the realization that he had but a handful of hours left to call this place his home. The swim back was made slower as Kahlen held his presents above his head and out of the water. Although Danielle swore that the bag was waterproof thanks to a foreign fabric covered with whale fat, Kahlen would not take the chance. As per the custom, when dawn came on your eighteenth name day and you were not married, you were either accepted into a new home as either husband or wife, brother or daughter and you were then to learn a new profession. Since it had been over three centuries since a member of the village received 'no-blessing' which is to say that no home would come forward to accept someone come of age, that Kahlen Bowsprit would become one of the 'cursed few' was as surprising as the sun rising in the West. Kahlen was, by all accounts, the strongest, kindest, and playfully earnest young man who was loved by all. He had never caused trouble and had properly courted Danielle in a time where couples would often sneak into the woods or onto boats to share themselves. To most, he was the obvious choice to wed Danielle and be trained as the new Dock Master which would also be akin to being a mayor. The Dock Master led the village in all things and his voice carried farthest and with the most weight. Also, as happens in most times, Kahlen and Danielle were also the prettiest couple and even the hardest of men could deny just how perfect they were together.

That is why, with less than two hours until dawn, Kahlen and Danielle sat in a protracted silence and stared at the horizon. "How come your father didn't name me, Danielle?" asked a visibly shaken Kahlen. He continued before Danielle could respond "Why? I mean I love you and your family. I always have. I have never turned my back on anyone who needed help. I have given myself to this village heart and soul. At the very least, your father should have named me just to make sure that you would be married to a man devoted to you and so that you would not have to go through the blessing next year." Danielle gently brushed the mop of hair from around his right eye and kissed Kahlen on the forehead. She pulled him closely and whispered "my love, when you asked my father for permission to court me last year he told you yes but he told me that night that no matter how I felt for you that if I truly loved you I would tell you that I wasn't interested. That losing your parents as a child was just the start of your burden. That life was not fair and that you would learn that more than any one person should have to."

Kahlen, sat there, wiping tears from his eyes and shook his head. "You've known for more than a year," he blurted. Kahlen's words were more of a statement than a question. He continued, "Did the whole village know?" Danielle stood and leaned against the porch rail and while holding back tears of her own added, "Yes. Some at least. The rest learned in the past few months. Only my father knows why. Or at least I think that he's the only one who knows why. I do know that the elders met several times in recent months and that no one has challenged his decision." As Kahlen felt his anger stir, he stood and took Danielle's hand in his own. He leaned his forehead onto hers and then kissed the top of her head. On the horizon, a pink hue began to claim the sky. Dawn was coming and soon Kahlen would be on his own. He could travel anywhere but he was sure that wherever he went he would never be home. Danielle nodded toward his sack full of gifts and hurried inside. Kahlen knew he had but a few minutes to make his way out of the village before the first breach of sunlight shone so he grabbed the cloth sack, cinched up the leather strap and hoisted it over his shoulder. As he stepped from the porch Danielle burst from the home and clutched Kahlen so tightly he had to remind himself to breathe. She held a simple burlap bag filled with nuts, berries and dried fish and meat. She kissed him one last time upon the lips and ran back inside her home.

Just like that, Kahlen Bowsprit was no more. He was one of the 'cursed few' and would never be allowed back in Crescent Bay. Now, he was just Kahlen. Kahlen the traveler. Kahlen the unworthy. Or more likely, Kahlen the lonely man killed by bandits. Kahlen never looked back. He had no desire to look ahead either but he was a prisoner to his feet and they kept moving forward.

In Crescent Bay, the village stirred and men were tending their ships, preparing for another day of fishing. Dock Master Averill waved the last of them off and after surveying the area headed back to his home. Sitting in his small kitchen with Danielle, he took out a parchment that was hidden behind a wooden panel next to the fireplace.

After reading it he stepped outside and waved the wet nurse Talia toward him. In hushed tones they spoke and then after handing her the parchment returned to his home. Once inside, the Dock Master faced his daughter whose face was full of questions. He sighed and spoke plainly. "We have done our duty, my daughter. That is all that I can say. At least today. Soon, I will explain it all. Just know that as much as we all loved Kahlen there was something bigger at stake." Averill knew his daughter would not accept his explanation and he could not blame her. She would understand, in time, but it wouldn't help today.

Talia had asked the stable master for a healthy mount and made her way down the Northern Trail. Some five miles outside of Crescent Bay, she came to a scryer's station. Hundreds of these stations exist throughout Tantra and although the buildings themselves are simple, the magic within is exotic. Each of these stations is capable of sharing information, for a price, with another station anywhere in the world. As Talia entered the station, a muscular man with a broadsword stood on guard. Talia opened the parchment toward the scryer and the man spotted the unmistakable mark of Prophet's Call. The scryer waved the guard aside and eagerly grabbed the parchment. He sniffed the paper and ran his finger over the embossed sigil. His fingers traced the curve of the blindfolded serpent which was not only a mark of Prophet's Call but the mark of the 'Dreamers', the society within the scryer's guild led by the Master of Spies; Duke Morecap.

The scryer invited Talia to his table and she sat beside him, facing an opaque pane of glass set between four brilliant gem stones. Talia had never seen such gems and she was so focused on them that she did not see the glass swirl and she did not see the image of Duke Morecap come into focus. She was startled when she heard the Duke speak. "Is the seal valid?" he asked. "Yes, master it is," replied the scryer. The Duke lifted his gaze and spoke directly to Talia. "Girl, are you from Crescent Bay?" "Yes, I am, Sir," Talia replied. The Duke continued, "Good, good. So, the boy has been shunned then?" Talia nodded and the Duke smiled before adding, "Now, it's very important that you return to your home and tell the Dock Master to bring the entire village together for my arrival in seven nights. I want you all there so I can explain how you may have saved all of Tantra. You and your people are heroes." Talia smiled as the glass turned cloudy again and she stood. She thanked the scryer and asked if she owed him any money. The scryer shook his head and said, "A scryer may live a dozen lifetimes and not speak with Duke Morecap directly. This moment was payment enough."

Talia climbed upon her horse and began the ride home. She had dreaded this day ever since Averill confided in her seven months ago that Kahlen must not receive a blessing for his name day. She had wept more frequently as this day drew closer. Now, after speaking with the Duke, she felt like there was a bigger purpose. She felt a sense of relief. She felt that she was part of something so important that the Duke considered them all heroes. Talia smiled at that thought. She was a hero.

3

Kahlen didn't look back. Not at first. He had traveled farther north than he had ever dared before. The way the light was diffused by the enormous trees made it difficult to gauge the time. He was sure it was past noon but he didn't know how late it might be. When he did look back he did not recognize the landscape. Thick, gnarled trees with white roots erupting from the ground in twisted agony, chased through the forest floor. The ground was a soggy mash of lichen and moss. The air felt damp and heavy. He could've traveled two miles or twenty. He had no idea but he knew that he was losing the day and a chill was sneaking under his skin.

Kahlen trudged on through the darkening woods occasionally reaching into the burlap bag for a handful of nuts. Sated, Kahlen started replaying the conversation he had with Danielle in his mind. The whole village knew. Everyone. Everyone but him. What could be so damned important that the very people he loved and had helped raise him when his parents died as a baby could turn him away? Kahlen kept questioning himself. He cried aloud at the thought that anything could be more important than supporting one of their own.

He swore and cursed the Gods. Kahlen leaned back to howl another curse and realized that he was so engrossed in self-pity that he never paid attention to how much day was left. He knew now that the sun was setting and night time would soon consume him. He kicked at the ground and punched the air at the realization that he had not prepared. Sobbing, Kahlen bowed his head, pressed his hand to the nearest tree and froze.

The tree was moving. Not the tree itself but the something or something's on the tree. Instead of bark he felt leather. Not smooth leather but a rugged kind with hints of rubbery veins. Kahlen reflexively pulled his hand from the tree and let out a less than heroic yelp. He stepped back; clutching the woven sack Danielle had gifted him and remembered the beautiful knife within. As he felt for the knife, Kahlen continued moving away from the tree only to back into another. This time something scrambled over his shoulder and through his hair and up the tree. His heart racing, panic setting in. Kahlen wanted to run, but run where? He thought. He didn't know his surroundings; he couldn't tell what direction he was facing. Kahlen was sure he was going to die in that copse of trees. Alone, his home and last name taken from him, Kahlen sat back down and pulled his knees to his chest. Kahlen instinctively waved the knife for a moment then it dawned on him that he hadn't even removed the sheath. The Knight of Crescent Bay was as useful as a fish out of water.

Above him, all around him really, the wind whipped. An eerie, high toned squeak shuttled from side to side, riding the wind. Kahlen pushed his face down, pressed it hard against his thighs and rocked back and forth. He had gripped the sheath so tightly his right hand felt bruised. The wind closed on him and something clipped his hair. He dropped the knife and it spilled from the sheath. Kahlen had survived sudden storm bursts outside of the Bay and had valiantly dove in to the raging sea to save a man thrown overboard by a violent wave. He had never felt this helpless. He had never felt so scared. With the defiant, anguished yell of a man facing certain death, Kahlen felt for his knife, brushed his fingers over the handle and secured it within his right hand. A blinding light shot from the handle, and exposed the terrors that swooped among the trees—Bats, the size of the largest gulls he had ever seen circled just beyond the light's reach. Kahlen stood with a sense of wonder, his fear ebbed and the light grew brighter. It also grew hotter. So hot in fact that the smoldering husks of the bats began dropping all around him. Kahlen switched his focus to the carcasses and so too did the light. A juvenile tree several feet away began to hiss and pop. Smoke billowed from the joints where branches met trunk. A spark and then a kiss of flames trickled upward. Kahlen sprung up and the light passed effortlessly through the elevated branches. Sure that the fire could not spread to another tree, Kahlen used the blade to cut the branches into smaller pieces to create a sustainable fire. There were few rocks but the thick moss was plentiful enough that Kahlen piled it all around the fire to help direct the heat. Kahlen sheathed the knife and pulled out a piece of dried fish and a handful of berries from his burlap bag. Sitting down, Kahlen glanced toward the knife and mumbled an apology to the Gods.

4

"How many men will we have for the morning?" King Corning asked. The King was standing at the war table, his hands cupping the rounded oak corners while his eyes surveyed the miniature figures that represented both armies. A member of his council, an aging governor whose best days were spent whoring his way through East Watch grumbled that "six thousand of our men were worth twenty thousand of those Southern hags". The King glanced briefly at the governor with a dismissive look and repeated, "How many men will we have for the morning?" This time, the council looked among themselves before Governor Adams, a simple man born into his position but well suited for common sense stepped to his King's side and offered, "We have four thousand infantry and another one thousand mounted. We have less than two hundred bowman and even if we had more, our fletchers cannot craft enough arrows. We had expected the two thousand men, mostly cavalry from Governor Sorling two days ago." Corning then asked Adams, "And what of that army approaching from the South?" Adams shrugged his shoulders and swung his head from side to side with a slight grimace.

He looked to the rest of his fellow council members for help but none would make eye contact.

The King slammed the pieces off of the table with a flourish. A stack of papers, mostly reports of dubious importance, fluttered around like the heavy snow that fell near the peaks of the Orphans. "Get Out!" the King screamed. "Get out and prepare your men. Prepare yourselves for each of you will be on the front, right by my side come dawn. Make your peace with God for tomorrow we will either step from the mud or die in it."

The council hurried from the tent but Governor Adams lingered just outside, still in view of the King. He stuck his head back inside the tent and exclaimed, "My liege, if you'd please? You must see this." King Corning, his interest piqued, stepped outside and uttered, "Mercy on us all." Set upon the ridge line stood two massive wooden figures. They were eighty, maybe one hundred feet tall. They were unmistakable. They were on fire. King Corning turned to Governor Adams. "Get me three riders. Also, get my historian and lastly, rouse General Krell. I think I know what we are facing."

5

"**W**hat the fuck is a Dagenskur?" Prince Oren asked incredulously. The old crone, considered insane by most and frightening by all, cleared her throat and explained. "The Dagenskur have not been seen in hundreds of years my Prince. What you see reaching to the stars are the Pyres of Woe."

"The Pyres of Woe?" sneered Prince Mallon. "It's fucking tall, I'll give them that. But why the fancy name?" The crone shuffled past the two princes and pointed a craggy finger toward the ridge. "Those effigies are how the Dagenskur let you know when your time has come. The fires burn until the last ember dies. Then, and only then, do they send for your most valorous man. The books of the First World told of how enemies would be vanquished in minutes. What is not known is why they come and why they choose to fight for one side or another. The old books say only that the worthy are chosen. It also says that the Dagenskur are the true protectors of Dorias. There was not much written in the last few hundred years however."

Oren and Mallon spoke in hushed tones while the camp stared at the raging fires. Even a mile or more away, the fire's heat could be felt in the camp. "It is decided," Oren called out. "I will go to them when the fire dies." The crone laughed. A guttural, phlegm coated laugh and she wagged the only working finger on her left hand. "No, no, no, my Prince I will not be your choice to make. They will choose and then either we will die or we will live." The crone hacked and wheezed her way through the assembled men. A sputtering laugh and then she turned to the Princes. A hush came over the men and her eyes lolled then went white. The crone sang quietly:

When the crown is tarnished
The land ruled by fear
Look to the East
For salvation's near
When the day does come
And our cries are heard
The just will prevail
They are the Dagenskur

Oren scoffed as the crone hobbled away. "I'm a Prince. Of course they'll pick me." Mallon banged his fist on Oren's shoulder and laughed. "If those crazy bastards think you are the most worthy then we've got nothing to worry about."

6

Upon the ridge, the Pyres of Woe burned and pieces of wood fell in charred lumps with a dull thud. Two hundred feet behind the Pyres sat a force of men, more than ten thousand in all. There were no adornments. There was hardly anything that resembled armor. There was no sign of horses or siege equipment. There was a sword and a spear lying in each man's lap. They all sat cross legged and were strangely barefoot. Each man was chanting in some unintelligible tongue but they were all in unison. They sat there, a subtle swaying in unison and the chant grew louder.

Hours passed and just before dawn the last remnant of fire went out. The Dagenskur stopped chanting and swaying. The two men sitting closest to the Pyres stood. As they rose, so too did the remainder of the army. The two men turned and faced the rest of the army and raised their hands to the sky. The army mimicked the movements and then stood still. The two men, indistinguishable from the rest by any standard other than their proximity to the pyres, stepped swiftly down the ridge. One made his way to Tantra's camp, the other to Wintersbane's.

. . .

King Corning had planned on sleeping. He had planned on many things in the thirty one years since he ascended the throne following his father's passing. Two months shy of his fiftieth name day, King Aticus Corning worried that he hadn't done enough to unite his divided country. He raced in time, searching for the meaning of so many decisions he'd made that led to this moment. Usually stout in his resolve, the King felt a twinge of doubt that maybe he was not worthy of his title. More than a twinge, maybe a convulsion.

The camp stirred and groaned to life as often happens in the short hours before dawn. Men who bragged about sleeping like a baby the night before going to war were usually the ones pissing themselves before buckling their sword belts. Devout men would often be found spilling out of the courtesan's tent just in case their prayers were not answered. Sober men would find a drink to their liking and then decide to have just one more until they emptied the bottle.

There is no wrong way to prepare to fight and likely die. These men, though, had been battling for nearly four straight days and usually that means the nervousness wears off a bit. This morning, even the most battle hardened veteran looked the part of a rookie. This morning, they stood within feet of legend and myth. This morning, the Dagenskur walked among them. The men of Tantra were terrified.

. . .

"So, our mighty Prince Mallon sure liked bringing up the rear today," laughed the Wintersbane camp guard to the stable hand. The boy looked around quickly before joining in on the laugh. The guard continued, "Of course that's still better than Oren and oy who goes there?" The Dagenskur soldier sized the guard and the boy and quickly dismissed them. The guard stepped in front of the soldier, hand on his sword hilt and yelled, "Enemy in the camp, Enemy in the camp". The Dagenskur soldier, expressionless, placed his hands outstretched and began chanting. The camp, now aware of the intrusion, rushed to the guardsmen's position. Oren and Mallon arrived to see their entire army standing, whispering among themselves. "Make way, boys," announced Oren. The men moved but never took their eyes off of the intruder. "I am Prince Oren and this is my brother Prince Mallon," started Oren. The Dagenskur soldier ceased chanting and his eyes darkened until there was no white left. In the early morning hours it was hard to tell if his eyes were there at all they had gone so black. The soldier turned slowly away from the Princes leaving them perplexed. The soldier raised his hand and a voice filled all of the Winterbane troop's minds. In their minds they could all hear, "Bring forward the man with the Old King's blood. Hair of clouds and face of tears." The words kept repeating until a man growled "I'm here, I'm here, and what do you ask of me?" Mallon leaned to Oren wondering, "Who is that?" Oren could only shrug his shoulders.

The voice changed and now they could all hear "You are the one named Roland. You are the descendant of Zion the Prosperous. You have been chosen." Roland, a stout man with pure white hair and three long, narrow scars descending from his left eye that looked very much like tears pursed his lips and nodded. "Okay, I'm chosen, now what?" The voice responded, "Now you decide your people's fate." Roland nodded at his Princes and Oren asked, "Who the hell are you, old man?" Roland said, "I'm just a soldier my Prince." "Just a soldier my ass," barked Mallon. Roland offered, "My bloodline has not been important for nearly three hundred years. Not since the rebellion led by your namesake, my Prince." The disembodied voice rattled the camp, "You have been Chosen, kin of Zion. You will come now." Roland raised his eyebrows and bowed his head slightly in deference to both Princes. Oren returned the gesture while Mallon shook his head with the hint of a wry, crooked smile. Roland stepped with the Dagenskur into the darkness outside of camp.

. . .

"Did you know that General Krell was of old blood, Governor Adams?" asked King Corning. Adams shook his head and said, "He never said anything to me. Quite frankly, the General didn't have much time with talking heads like me. He did tell me once after a battle two years ago that his voice only mattered to his men and that's why he never tried to talk strategy with the council." The King was partly amused at the turn of events and partly worried that his best General carried within him the blood of the family his own deposed. "Saddle my horse," the King called out and footsteps could be heard scrambling toward the stables.

. . .

Oren and Mallon and about twenty personal guards trotted to the center of the battlefield where King Corning and a small retinue waited, a flag of truce in hand. Mallon spoke first, "You and the rest of your toy soldiers ready to quit?" The Wintersbane troops chortled at the jest. Corning turned his attention from Mallon to Oren and began, "Have you had a champion chosen yet?" Oren responded tersely "Aye". "As have we," finished Corning. "Are you worried that your man isn't worth? Are you here to run away and hope those black eyed bastards will just go away?" interjected Mallon. "On the contrary, boys. I am confident that my man, a man of old king's blood will be worthy. I simply wish to cease hostilities until, as you say, those bastards choose." "Of course, if you wanted to bend the knee and accept me as your one true king," smirked Corning. Oren laughed mockingly and said, "We will hold off killing you now because when we are deemed worthy I'll sit here by Mallon's side and watch your army get blown into history. Let's go." As he guided his horse around, Mallon added, "Oh, and Corning, old blood runs deep in the South too.

Maybe you should bend your knee." Mallon and the rest did not wait to hear Corning's response. They raced back to camp to celebrate the victory to be.

The King figured that dawn was only twenty minutes away. He sipped his tea and decided, while removing a large plug capped decanter from his trunk, that there would be nothing wrong with adding a splash of his favorite drink. A drink, he considered, made from water from the Old Warrior, rye from south of the Range, and fermented fruit only found in the tropics. The same tropics where his snot nosed enemies hailed from. Where their father Marcus Ottrun was born some forty odd years ago and not surprisingly, where he was found dead two years ago. Corning always suspected one of the sons responsible but there was no evidence to connect either. He mused that if only he had a magical way to dispose of them himself and allowed himself a quick derisive laugh. The damned Dagenskur were real. They were real and they were here. They were here and he did not know if this would be his last dawn. Corning took a deep breath then slid his tea aside and took a long, lusty swallow from the decanter instead.

7

Upon the ridge, past the cold bits of charcoal and ash that sat where the two raging pyres were lit just hours before, stood General Edmund Krell and arms man Roland Cain. The two men traded glances at first and then nods and then as if prodded spoke simultaneously. Chagrined, General Krell asked, "May I?" Roland acquiesced. Krell began, "I apologize, Sir. I am not familiar with you. I am General Edmund Krell, primary commander of the King's royal forces. And you are?" Roland pushed his shirt sleeve up to his elbow and made a point of showing the cross and dagger tattoo that was the only link to his more famous ancestors. "My, my," said Krell. "You are truly from the House of Cain?" "Yes, Sir. I am the blood of Zion Cain and his descendants. I'll be the last though. My wife and child died years ago at sea and a well-placed spear soon after ensured that the line would end with me."

Krell took a moment to reassess his foe. He seemed the serious sort. The man who knew his duty and performed it well under pressure. He tried to ignore the fact that Cain was the only man between victory and death. He instantly liked Roland Cain. "You look at me like I'm a suckling pig," cracked Roland. Both men laughed and instinctively patted each other on the shoulder. "So, Ed, some fairy tales come true eh?" asked Roland. "So it would seem, Roland. So. It. Would. Seem," replied Krell. Both men stopped talking as the Dagenskur rose to listen to what the two leaders had to say. To Krell and Cain, it sounded like a sing song cacophony of guttural sounds mixed with a flitting tease of harmony. It made both men uneasy and they exchanged a silent nod before focusing on the force before them. If these men were going to die, they sure as hell weren't going to give the other any satisfaction. No pleading for mercy. No whining about wanting to live. No chance for one to lose the respect of the other. They both thought that at any other time, they would have made great friends.

When the sky changed from black to pink neither man could tell. The pink deepened and an orange hue melted in as the sun began to edge over the horizon. Krell likened the colors to the frozen custard treat he loved as a child. Cain, on the other hand, thought the smudges looked much like the make up the first whore he ever visited, wore. Both men were smiling at their thoughts when the two men, undoubtedly the leaders by how the others responded to them, approached. The Dagenskur spoke into Krell's and Cain's minds. The words were clear. The Dagenskur were here to maintain the peace of the land. They were called upon to ensure that no person or people became too powerful. The Dagenskur were in essence the scale by which Dorias would remain balanced.

Krell's mind raced and he thought to himself, "Why are we here. What need do you have of us?" Cain added, "Yeah, how does this work?" The Dagenskur shared the thought, "You are both of old blood. From the last time we were here. Your blood will tell who is worthy of us or not." Krell kept questioning "how will our blood tell? What happens if one is worthy? What happens if one is not?" The Dagenskur looked at each other silently, little to no facial expressions to gauge what effect the questions had. The Dagenskur gathered their thoughts and explained, "We will know which foe worthy of being is struck down in battle. To face their end at our hand is the greatest gift we could give. If unworthy, then they will be left to their own devices. They will know that they are to care for their own and grow stronger. To become worthy. Not to conquer. To respect the balance."

Krell and Cain were released from the thought connection with the Dagenskur and could no longer hear each other's thoughts. To the men, there was great relief as secretly, they both hoped to be the most unworthy wretch to have ever walked the earth.

8

The fishermen had just returned with various successes. An unexpected swell accompanied by high winds and intermittent downpours prevented the men from reaching some of their favorite and plentiful fishing locations. The sky, full of thunder, its color swirling between a hazy pink and an ominous purplish black, hung like a soggy cloak just above Crescent Bay. Dock master Averill had just finished collecting his weekly mooring fee from each of the returning men. Unlike the practices in most ports, the fee here is more of a simple tribute. Since all men and women in the village support each other with goods and services, there is no coin used within the village. The men and women offer a small part of whatever they acquire or produce or catch. Every item paid went into the storehouse for anyone to use. Averill would, as was his right, take just enough for Danielle to prepare for dinner. Coin is reserved for the trading trips to North Watch down the Northern Trail. On special occasions, when the fishing is bountiful or when something special is needed, a brave few would make the long trip through the Green Sea to East Watch. There have been whispers that two years ago, Averill had left on a trading mission to East Watch and inexplicably ended up in Blackstone. There was never any acknowledgment of that from Averill, but the ship full of iron tools and weapons took the entire village to unload and required seven cart loads to bring to North Watch. For the better part of two weeks, a procession of goods made its way back to the village with cloth, coin, wine, rope, canvas, and one hand signed note of gratitude signed by Duke Morecap.

Averill had stepped back into his home to find Talia sitting with Danielle. Talia smiled and said, "Everyone knows to be ready tomorrow, Dock master." "Fine, fine work, Talia," replied Averill. "Would you like some wine, father?" asked Danielle. In the six days since he had ensured the village's future by banishing Kahlen, Danielle had not given hint to her emotions. Surely, he thought, Danielle would have threatened to run away or skip the threat and banish herself. Instead, she showed the resolve and the maturity of a woman twice her age and accepted the decision, hard as it was, as it was for the greater good. Averill knew that this young woman who stood before him would, in time, be the kind of leader that would ensure his lineage remained the Dock master for generations to come.

As the sky sagged, heavy with rain that threatened the village, a rider approached. A tall man, riding high in the saddle with his left hand resting on his left thigh and the reins held loosely in his right. He passed the stables and rode the horse into the village center where he dismounted and tied the horse to a post. The rider turned his gaze to Averill and smiled. Duke Morecap arrived a day too soon.

"May I come in, Dock master?" asked the Duke. Stammering a bit, Averill responded nervously "Yes, of course. Please, come in. Looks like rain." Duke Morecap strode purposefully into the Dock master's home and made himself at home. He tossed his riding cloak over the first chair he saw and grabbed the bottle of wine and sniffed it. He searched for a glass and when he found one that wasn't excessively dirty, he poured in the wine and sipped it. Satisfied that this wine came from one of Tantra's western vineyards and thus palatable, he drank the cup down. Pouring himself another cup, the Duke motioned for Averill to take a seat at his own table and asked, "Where is your young one, Dock master?" Averill, turned his head slightly as if not understanding the question and then with a start, "Danielle, love, please come meet our guest."

Danielle approached the table and with her eyes averted out of respect welcomed the Duke with a curtsy. The Duke told Danielle to stand and to join them at the table. Danielle looked at her father for approval but the Duke said simply, "You do not need permission, my lady. I have requested your presence and I am certain that your father would not mind." Danielle sat to the Duke's right and watched him finish another cup of wine. After the Duke asked Averill to fetch some bread to go with the wine, he leaned toward Danielle, "You, my dear, are a lovely sight. I had no idea that a woman of your beauty could come from such common stock." Averill bristled at the comment but said nothing as he brought a loaf of bread to the Duke. After he returned to his seat, Averill asked the Duke if Talia had misunderstood the directives. The Duke assured Averill that Talia did as she was told and that he did indeed want the village to expect him tomorrow.

The hair on the back of Averill's neck stood at the sound of the shrill scream. Averill darted a look to the Duke and then pushed away from the table. The Duke, still chewing a piece of bread, wagged his finger in the manner a parent would to a child that says 'don't do that'. Averill, his face tortured with angst, whipped the door open only to be forcibly escorted back to the table by soldier. "What is going on?" Averill pleaded with the Duke. The Duke paused to use his bread crust to soak up the remaining drops of wine from his cup before answering, "I, my good Dock master, am concluding our bargain." "Bargain?" said the incredulous Averill. "Bargain!" Averill continued with anger. "Who is being hurt out there? Why? We've done all you've asked. We've never betrayed your trust."

The Duke stood, the chair sliding back seemingly on its own. The Duke probed his teeth with his tongue to dislodge a piece of bread that wedged itself annoyingly near an incisor and after smacking his lips returned his attention to Averill. "The screams," the Duke started, "are of the fine villagers of Crescent Bay who you should know are not being hurt...they are being executed." Tears, anger, and grief overwhelmed Averill and he pounded his fist on the table with such force that the soldier outside stormed in to protect the Duke. The Duke let the soldier know "I am quite fine. Please, return to your post." The soldier saluted with his hand to his chest, pivoted, and went outside. The soldier secured the door shut and the Duke chuckled. More screams, the neighing of horses, and then an eerie calm beset the village. Averill was leaning against the door and remembered the scroll the Duke had given him eighteen years earlier.

"Danielle," spat Averill. "Go to the desk and retrieve the scroll with the red dagger seal." Maybe it was the fact that Averill was facing his own mortality with a decided certainty. Maybe Averill was simply being defiant and stubborn. Whatever the cause, Averill steeled himself with some well of nerve. Averill glared at the Duke who returned the look with one of vague curiosity. Danielle stopped short of handing her father the scroll and looked to the Duke for a sign of permission. "Don't stop on my account," the bemused Duke said. Averill snatched the scroll and read it. Certain that he had been wronged; the Dock master sneered at the Duke and tapped the scroll with his finger. "I thought you were a man of your word, Morecap," challenged Averill.

His interest piqued, the Duke churned Averill's pot by asking him to "please continue." Averill, emboldened, continued. "Right here is your seal. These are your words are they not?" The Duke peered at the scroll and said "they are." "So, you agree these are your words and that means you are to uphold these words, Duke," Averill raged. The Duke bowed with a flourish and after an extended time replied, "Averill, I have fulfilled my end of the bargain to its fullest. In our agreement, Crescent Bay was to care for the child I came to you with and to cast him out on his eighteenth name day.

In exchange, while you cared for the boy, you and your meager little fish mongers would profit immeasurably at the trade markets, you would find your travels unimpeded even when violating the Queen's law by venturing to Blackstone. Most importantly, I promised, no, I guaranteed that your village would be free from conscription or rebuke from the Queen's army."

Averill, his resolve waning, looked from the scroll to the Duke and back again. Feeling despair set in he grasped at one more straw. "My people are all dead. Your words are meaningless. The Queen's army is here and we are all dead." The Duke put his index finger to Averill's lips and stinking of wine breathed these words. "Yes, your people are all dead, that much is true. But, Dock master, that is not the Queen's army. My word is my bond."

Averill didn't feel the blade slide between his ribs until it struck bone. Grunting, Averill feebly grabbed the hilt to find Danielle's hand still firmly attached. A look that was a mix of sorrow and confusion passed briefly over Averill's face before he collapsed lifelessly, blood pooling on the floor. Danielle stared at the body for a moment and then raised her eyebrow before brushing herself off. "Are you ready to go, my dear?" Morecap asked Danielle. "I've been ready since the day I met you," she purred.

9

Kahlen had walked; more like willed his way through the thickening forest. In the month since he had left Crescent Bay, Kahlen had found his way to the base of one of the smaller mountains that made up the Orphans. A cascade of jagged rock with a peak lost so high in the sky that the clouds couldn't fly high enough to clear it. The wind was much different here. It sang. It sang in a mournful wail that reminded Kahlen of the stories of the sirens at sea. While he was pretty sure he couldn't drown here, he'd thought it best to try and ignore the song just the same. The ground was a patchwork of dried grasses and pine cones was always cold to the touch. The wood was the hardest he had ever felt and wondered how strong a ship could be built with it. Game was plentiful and with his remarkable knife, he never went without a warm fire. Kahlen had decided that he would follow the sun while skirting the mountains. He hoped that he would pass a road or village or even a game trail. Instead, he traversed a craggy, hardscrabble, pock marked series of slopes and inclines that directed him further into the wilderness. Kahlen stopped more frequently to follow the sun and to unleash the power of the blade.

Although Kahlen knew that there would be the first hint of color to the leaves in and around Crescent Bay, here, there was only green upon the trees. The nights had begun to grow cold enough that Kahlen created multiple fires to surround himself with at night. If it grew any colder before he found a safe haven, he feared that the blade alone would not be able to save him. His clothes had worn in the knees and his boots had small holes in them. It would not be long, he surmised, until he would be so exposed to the elements that sickness would set in. As night grew closer, Kahlen unsheathed his blade and created five small fires in a rough circle around where he chose to bed. As the last of the fires crackled to life, another, louder, cracking sound echoed from nowhere and everywhere all at once. Kahlen spun around and trained his ear in the general direction he felt the sound came from. He heard nothing at first. Then, a grunt just outside of his ring of fire made Kahlen wheel in the opposite direction. "Stand back," Kahlen nervously hollered. Kahlen stammered, "I don't want any trouble."

No words rang out from the bushes. No challenges. Just a grunt. Then, Kahlen saw the eyes. He squinted, his focus on two large eyes glowing reddish black thanks to the fires. Kahlen had heard how large bears could grow but he couldn't remember a time seeing one when he wasn't on board a fishing ship and the bear safely on land. Bears seemed far less daunting when sailing. They seemed like a pet you could call home for dinner. The reality was far more threatening. This bear grunted and sniffed the air. The bear moved slowly toward the fire and sniffed multiple times before locking its gaze on Kahlen. Kahlen stared back briefly and then reached for his blade. The bear then shook its head at Kahlen, grunted and laid down next to the fire. Within minutes, the bear was asleep. Kahlen secured his pack over his shoulder, placed the blade within its sheath and then into his pocket. Kahlen wrestled with the thought that he should just use the blade to kill the bear. The idea of food and fur had him leaning one way. The idea that maybe this was a sign to move on had him slinking quietly in the other direction. He simply hoped that when dawn came he would be in a better place.

Dawn came and went three more times before he saw it. He wasn't sure what it was, but in his heart he knew it was, well, something. Kahlen regretted letting the bear live a few nights earlier as two toes were clearly visible where leather used to be wrapped around his right foot. He longed for the sea, the warm moist air and the lapping of the waves. He chastised himself for choosing to go north instead of South or West. He just didn't want to go where there was a chance of coming across someone from the Bay. Kahlen shivered and redirected his attention on the odd rocks strewn on and around a small mound of earth. Some forty yards away from the site, Kahlen recognized one of the stones. They were the same as from the Bay Heart. These rocks were part of another temple. Kahlen had found another ruin of the First World. Kahlen forgot about being cold and hungry. Kahlen moved swiftly about the area and crested the mound. In his pocket, the blade shook itself out of his pocket and fell with a low thud to the ground. Wide eyed, Kahlen warily pulled it out of its sheath. There was a low hum to go with the shaking and he could feel something pulling the blade away from him. Kahlen loosened his grip slightly, but not enough to let go of it. The blade turned in his hand ever so slightly and Kahlen moved in that direction. As he walked, the blade turned a couple of times altering Kahlen's path. Kahlen felt the pull strengthen as he neared a second, smaller mound that was hidden behind the first mound.

The blade stood in the palm of his hand and started spinning. It was a slow, wobbly spin at first. Eventually, the spin tightened and turned so quickly that it bruised Kahlen's hand and he dropped the blade. The blade landed, hilt first, and continued to spin. Flame light erupted from the hilt and Kahlen dove to safety. Kahlen didn't know how long he lay at the base of the hill but instinctively, he rose and worked his way back up to his blade. Kahlen stared in disbelief as his blade was gone and so too was the top of the hill. Instead of earth there was a hole wider than he was tall. Kahlen knelt beside the hole and nervously spied within. In the hole there was a twinkling of light and maybe fifteen feet down lay his blade. As his eyes adjusted, he could see shapes of people. And he thought he heard water running. To his left, Kahlen spotted steps carved into the rock within the hole. Kahlen turned over and slid feet first into the hole until he touched stone. When he was sure that the stone could hold his weight, he edged downward until he could use the small steps like a ladder. Seconds later, Kahlen reached the floor but instead of dirt there was more stone. His blade lay motionless upon the floor.

Kahlen now knew that the shapes of the people he saw from above were fully articulated statues. They were of a polished stone and within the stone there was something that sparkled and dappled as light struck it. Within these ruins, Kahlen felt calm and safe. There was a strange warmth within as well and a curious series of images of a one legged man doing various things along one side of the room. The two most interesting images were of the man with a woman and child inside a fort or castle followed by the man holding the child while a wolf stood beside them. Kahlen stepped toward the blade and it slid several feet away. He moved toward it and again it darted away. Kahlen was more amused with his blade's new found life than alarmed by it. He pretended to not be interested in the blade and turned his back on it. Kahlen turned and dove headfirst toward the blade, but landed with a thud and empty handed. A small clanking just ahead of him in a little alcove off of this main room alerted Kahlen to his blade's position. Crouching, he reached out with his hands into the darkened room and inched forward.

The room erupted in light and before Kahlen rested he saw a casket of clear glass and within lay a man so well preserved that Kahlen would not be surprised if he sat up and said hello. Under the casket was a slab of stone that Kahlen recognized as the altar from the Bay Heart. That meant that at some point, someone important was once buried in the Bay. There was no way to identify the man before him but Kahlen felt compelled to touch the casket. Kahlen gently rested his right hand upon the casket's top and the top shimmered before sliding away into nothingness. Kahlen jerked back reflexively and muttered an exclamation under his breath. Within the casket there were two items which Kahlen felt drawn toward. One was a small locket of gold and sapphires. When Kahlen pressed the clasp of the locket it opened easily to reveal two apparently empty halves. There was a subtle shimmering within the locket that Kahlen accepted as a trick of the eye. Kahlen turned the locket in his hand and engraved in its case were the words; Purity, Balance and Rebirth. Kahlen turned the locket back over and closed it shut. Kahlen felt sadness for this stranger and placed the locket as close to where he found as he could. Kahlen glanced at the second item of interest, an ornate staff about four and half feet long with the same sparkling effect as found within the statues in the next room. Kahlen lifted the staff and marveled at how light it was. At one end there was a slotted opening with a raised ring and at the other end, a prismatic crystal that seemed to have captured every color in the world and trapped them within. Kahlen held the staff in one hand, marveling at its weight and tried to squeeze it. The staff was solid and unyielding. He grabbed it with both hands and swung it like a sword and it moved effortlessly. It was so well balanced and light—it felt natural to hold. Kahlen sighed and went to place the staff back in the casket when his blade sang and light spread from it, cascading over the staff.

Kahlen stepped near his blade and it moved toward him. Another step and the closer the blade moved. Kahlen was close enough to bend down and reach the blade but before he could move any closer, the blade flew upward and secured itself into the base of the staff with an audible click. Kahlen watched the hilt twist to the right and a soft glow pulsed inside the staff, moving upward until it swirled within the crystal itself. Kahlen tried to unscrew the blade from the staff but failed. Frantic, Kahlen feared that he would be helpless without the blade. He felt terribly about what he was about to do but he knew that he would need that blade so he slammed the staff on the edge of the altar. The staff passed through the altar without a sound. He felt no contact. Kahlen began questioning if he missed the altar altogether. Kahlen swung more ferociously and again the staff passed through the altar. Befuddled, Kahlen looked up at the ceiling and absentmindedly tapped the base of the staff on the floor. The crystal atop the staff blossomed in light and intensified in the direction Kahlen focused. Kahlen glanced from side to side and the light mimicked his focus. Kahlen stepped from the alcove and faced a statue of a woman holding a book above her head and a child hugging her leg. Kahlen focused intently on the book and the light narrowed to match his focus. The light bore a hole through the book. Kahlen turned back into the alcove to apologize to the gods and to the man whose grave he just robbed. Kahlen stopped abruptly as the casket sat empty save for the golden locket. The locket sat on its edge and was open. The right half of the locket remained empty but from the left half stared a face Kahlen knew immediately; it was his own.

10

Two Dagenskur soldiers carried a wide wooden plank above their heads and after walking behind Krell and Cain, and set the plank to the ground. There were ropes in loops at five positions on the board. Krell cocked his head from one side to the other and understood the meaning. Cain chuckled and said, "Looks like they're aiming to take a little target practice, heh." Krell turned to Cain and with a wink said "and here comes your ride" as two more soldiers walked behind them with another board. This one, like the other had loops of rope. The reddish hue had dissipated and most of the sun was visible over the horizon. The two Dagenskur leaders approached and in their heads, Krell and Cain could hear, "The worthy shall be known. Purity of soul, Balance of Nature, Rebirth of the First World." As if entranced, Krell and Cain willfully allowed the Dagenskur to ease them to the ground and tie them to the boards. One loop for each wrist and ankle. The last around the neck. The boards were lifted into a standing position and the ropes were pulled taut. As tough as Krell and Cain were, there was no mistaking the scent of loose bowels as the massive army closed ranks and began to chant. To anyone in either camp the chant was indecipherable rabble. Loud and foreboding, but merely noise. To Krell and Cain, their minds connected to the Dagenskur in some mystical way, all they heard were, "We search the worthy. Purity. We protect the land. Balance. We prepare for the return of the First World. Rebirth."

A loud roar of what could only be described as joy reverberated from the Dagenskur. The Sun had risen fully and the two leaders, one facing Krell the other facing Cain, produced a glistening blade of black steel and without word or emotion proceeded to carve each man's heart from their chest in a single stroke. The leaders held the hearts up to the army and watched the hearts beat; once, twice, and then a third time each. The leaders bit into each heart and screamed a war cry. If Krell or Cain were alive to hear the next chant they would've heard "Both are Worthy. Both are worthy. Prepare for Balance."

. . .

King Corning didn't need his advisors to tell him that the Dagenskur were prepared for war. The blood thirsty roar that surged from just above the ridge was more than enough proof. He adjusted his belt and closed his eyes. One deep breath later, the King strode defiantly from his tent and commanded his troops to the ready. Atop his horse, the King rode to the battlefield and turned his mount first toward the forces from Wintersbane and then to his own troops, now massed and at the ready. The King bellowed for his advisors to march at his side and they did. Some, eager and willing, most reticent and slower to appear but appear they did. The king trotted back and forth, sitting as tall as he could in the saddle. He made a point to acknowledge his men's bravery and even tried his best to call to individuals by name in order to buck up their confidence. Upon his return to the center of the line and his expectant advisors, the King chided the brothers Oren and Mallon as being "late to the party...as usual". The King's staff tittered nervously at the quip and then Governor Adams took it upon himself to shout it out to the rest of the men and a hearty laugh was the response.

The king spoke to the assembled leadership calmly and directly. "This will either be our finest hour or our last, gentlemen. Regardless of the outcome, know this, we fight to unite Dorias. To bring the South not to heel, but into our bosom. To create one land with one rule. A stronger, united land to last the next thousand years." These men, rich aristocrats and Governors all, not normally given to patriotic fervor, cheered their King and for a brief moment allowed themselves some prideful hope.

• • •

Mallon kicked Oren's foot as it dangled from his bed. It was a woman who sat up with a randy "coming to join us, my Prince?" After shepherding the whore out of the tent, much to Oren's dismay, the two shared a flagon of their private stock of ale. There was an unusual silence as they drank. The men seemed to be savoring the drink and were in no hurry to drink the flagon dry. When, at last, they did drink it down, the men grabbed their favorite weapons and headed to the stables. Oren, wearing a simple shirt and pants, muddy boots, and a knowing smile peered at the assembled Tantra forces across the field and spat. Mallon, in full traditional armor with a fur overcoat pulled his hair back and tied it with a strip of cloth. They both climbed aboard a ready steed and Mallon leaned back spotted Timbor fastening his sword to his belt and nonchalantly told him to "assemble the men". Within two minutes, the fighting men of Wintersbane had more or less presented themselves ready for war. One man stood naked save for his sword and shield. Cheeky comments begat more ribald ones and soon everyone had chimed in. Even Oren, who brought his horse to bear in front of the clothing challenged man had to ask, "Are you so brave or stupid?" The man pushed his chest out and replied, "I am a bit of both. But I am your brave and stupid man, my Prince." Laughing, Oren answered, "Yes, yes you are but if it gets any colder they may think a woman is charging them".

Oren brought his horse aside Mallon's and asked, "So, what do you think will happen brother?" Mallon glanced sideways and with a shrug said, "I think, dear brother, that many good men will die today." and after pausing a bit finished his statement. "And I think many of those snotty pricks over there will die too." With the smile still on his lips he heard the rhythmic chant from the Dagenskur. His mood spoiled, Mallon stole a look at Corning across the field that appeared unaffected by the arrival of the Dagenskur. "Here they come," a hushed Oren whispered. "Yes, Oren," replied Mallon. Mallon paused before finishing. "Here They. Come."

· · ·

The Dagenskur spread in formation spanning the entirety of the ridge line. Even without cavalry or bowmen, the sheer number of infantry dwarfed the combined forces of Tantra and Wintersbane. Some twenty to twenty five thousand men stood barefoot, a small, dual edged sword in the right hand and a thick spear in their left. The base of each spear was six inches of black steel, thicker than the body and jutted at an angle. For the Dagenskur, this design has two purposes; one purpose is for balance when preparing to commence an aerial assault and the other purpose is to allow for a quick defensive posture when preparing for an onslaught of cavalry. The Dagenskur can either stand upon the angled piece or drive it directly into the turf and wait for a horse to impale itself. The Dagenskur held neither shields nor armor. The flaps of cloth and animal hide they wore did little more than cover their manhood. They were not of this time. They were primordial. They were death incarnate.

In step, the Dagenskur flowed down the hill toward the center of the battlefield. The armies of Tantra and Wintersbane edged back toward their respective camps. Not retreating but not willing to engage the foreign warriors. The Dagenskur were still trailing over the ridge, the grasses blotted by the humanity...if they were indeed human. The lead soldiers came to a stop and as the remaining soldiers closed, they too stopped in formation. The procession lasted for several minutes and when finished, the singing began. A lilting, haunting song. A song that was as beautiful as it was mournful. If this was a song sung by the entertainers from Freeman's Point the audience would be brought to tears and wild applause. Even in the strange tongue, the meaning was clear; this was a song of renewal. A song of loss. A song of finality.

The song ended and one Dagenskur faced the rest and raised both weapons as if in offering. The rest of the army mirrored the pose and in unison pivoted to face King Corning and his men. Throughout the field, all men could hear a low buzzing in their ears and then this: "The choice is made. Purity of blood, need of Balance, hope from Re-Birth. You are worthy."

The deafening roar from behind the King drowned out the sickening exhalation coming from bewildered Wintersbane troops. King Corning turned his mount and smiled at his men. He patted Governor Adams on his breastplate and said, "I will welcome our new allies, personally." The King snapped his stallion into a hard run and pulled up the reins just shy of the first row of the Dagenskur. The King joyously exclaimed "On behalf of..." The spear split the King's skull before he could finish his greeting. Spilled from his horse, the King of Tantra lay dead. The Dagenskur started jogging toward the rudderless army, scattered cries from within the ranks led to confusion and by the time Governor Adams seized the opportunity to take command, it was over. The Dagenskur engulfed Tantra's forces and closed down like a hungry wolf on a wounded lamb.

Across the field, Oren and Mallon sat silently upon their horses. Where moments earlier there were tears and mournful wails given that the horde descending from the ridge had call Tantra worthy there now was laughter and cheers. Their morale returned, excitement arose from the knowledge that the old stories had it wrong. The worthy weren't aided by the Dagenskur; they were swatted like a fly. "It looks about finished I think," an awestruck Oren opined. Mallon, feeling his oats, told Oren, "I think we should decide who goes with the main force to Tantra. The sooner one of us takes their throne the better it will be." "Well, I've always wanted to have a turn or two with those highborn at court," chuckled Oren. "Then, it's agreed. You can rule Tantra and I will stay and keep Wintersbane," decided Mallon. Oren, consternation seeping over his brow, asked carefully, "Now, shouldn't there be just one ruler in Dorias?" Mallon sidled his horse close to Oren's and placed his hand on Oren's knee. "Brother, between the two of us, we barely hold our own land together. How could we hope to hold all of Dorias together if only one of us ruled?" Mallon continued, "We are about to have the world handed to us by creatures who stepped from the storybooks. We can take a moment and discuss this further if you'd like."

As the dust settled on the far side of the battlefield, Mallon and Oren could see that the Dagenskur were reforming ranks. As Mallon scanned the carnage he couldn't help but notice that all of the casualties seemed to be from Tantra. He often mocked the courage of those men, now dead, carrion already descending from the sky to pick the bones clean. He always knew that they were well trained and brave. He knew they had families and lives that didn't always involve blood and steel. He knew that those men fought with fierceness. All of that and not a single Dagenskur lay dead. He saw no wounded being attended to either. None. Mallon felt small at the realization that what he witnessed was not the result of man but of magic. Old magic. He felt small with the knowledge that no one knew the truth of the Dagenskur.

The Dagenskur were walking deliberately in their direction and Mallon made eye contact with Oren and then nodded his head toward the oncoming men. The two men spurred their horses into a trot and pushed forward until they were a third of the way to the Dagenskur. Oren stroked his horse's mane and clucked his tongue on the roof of his mouth trying to settle the beast which pulled and reared as the Dagenskur approached. "It's okay, boy. There, there." Oren cooed to his horse, turning his attention to Mallon. "Mallon, seems we can take that moment, now." Flabbergasted, Mallon chirped back. "Now? I think we are just minutes away from ruling the world. It can wait."

Oren moved his horse closer to Mallon's and placed his left hand on Mallon's shoulder and began. "Mallon, my dear brother, this is the perfect time you see, father's dream was to stand as the King of all the world. He never gave us any thought. As a matter of fact, our dear father planned on taking a new wife. Some whore from Tantra and he was going to spend as much time as it took to get another son. That's when we wouldn't be needed anymore." Mallon took a furtive glance toward the Dagenskur who were within shouting distance now and then back to Oren who he asked, "Why would you say this? Father never would've cast us aside. He was our father. How dare you?"

Oren tipped his head back and turned side to side. His neck popped and cracked and caused an involuntary shiver that elicited a: whoop' noise that sounded like it came out of his nose. Oren gave a shake of his head that spoke of disappointment and discouragement. "Do you know why I spent so much time whoring and drinking, Mallon? Well, when men drink they share more information than they planned to. Men also make the mistake of telling whores way too much information whether or not they are any good in bed. So, I decided that I'd play the stupid brother. The brother who, wait for it, drank too much and whored too much. The brother who learned of the truth and decided to do something about it." Mallon, breathing hard, worry of the unknown weighing him down in the saddle choked out the words. "Oren, what do you mean that you decided to do something about it?" Oren opened his mouth wide in mock surprise and said in a disturbingly effusive tone, "I killed him. I knew where he was going to be and used my drinking friends to entertain his guards and when my whore had tied him to the bed as was his like, I came in and slit his throat."

Mallon was so hurt and surprised by what he had heard that he never saw the blade slide out of Oren's left sleeve and into the hand that still held onto Mallon's saddle. He looked even more surprised when Oren wrenched his hand from the saddle and plunged the blade so deep into Mallon's neck that it burst through the other side with a wet, sucking sound. Oren pulled the blade back out and wiped it off on Mallon's shirt sleeve before pushing Mallon off of his horse. Mallon's horse jumped and backed away at the sound of his body thumping to the ground. Oren, lost in some wistful thought, was struck by reality as the Dagenskur halted, inches from his horse.

As Oren was about to talk, his ears began to buzz and he could hear clearly, "The choice is made. Purity of blood, need of Balance, hope from Re-Birth. You are worthy." Oren tried to swear but his head was lopped from his shoulders in an instant and with it all of his machinations.

In camp, the assembled men, most still at the ready, others celebrating what moments ago seemed like a victory had difficulty making out what was happening between the Princes. They were even more confused when Mallon fell from his horse. Clarity sprung from the next event; Oren's head spun to the ground coming to rest beside his brother. By the time the men of Wintersbane were able piece it all together, the Dagenskur was upon them. The men brought their weapons to bear and blow certain to kill or maim simply passed through the Dagenskur. These men didn't just bring death with them, they were death. Death and shadows.

• • •

When the last Wintersbane soldier died, the Dagenskur chanted three words; Purity, Balance, Rebirth. The Dagenskur reformed into marching lines and headed toward the horizon. Mere seconds passed and then the Dagenskur disappeared into nothing.

11

"If they all died then how do we know what happened?" asked Catherine Sorling, second surviving daughter of the late King Terrence Sorling and next in line to the throne of Tantra. Sitting atop a stack of large pillows, fresh ink in a well to her right and a writing table on her lap covered with paper and quills, the Princess pressed her tutor for an answer. "Well," she nudged, "how do we know that any of this happened?" Catherine, who preferred being called Cat stretched her foot and dug her toe into her younger sister's side. Rose, who only heard that name when she was in trouble, had gone by the nickname Mouse for as long as she could remember. Mouse yelped in surprise as Cat's toe dug into her ribcage and agreed with her big sister. "Yes, Ms. Boson is it real?" Ms. Boson, a long faced woman with eyebrows permanently elevated so that she always looked like she was in a state of surprise, cleared her throat gently and replied. "Ladies, I will tell you what I told our Queen." The girls sat up as Ms. Boson settled near them within the pillows. Ms. Boson continued, "The events of the Great War for Dorias are true. The reports of what happened are taken directly from the written reports given to your ancestor the estimable Governor Mandrake Sorling. You see, Governor Sorling was expected to arrive as the primary reinforcement for old King Corning but smartly chose to stay camped in the old ruins just south of what we now call Splendor."

"You mean he let them die? He was a coward?" chirped Mouse. "No, no, dear. He was a very smart man. He was the Governor of the West and lived near Prophet's Call. He had grown up with men and women, servants and suitors alike that dabbled in magic. Your family history shows that Mandrake would visit the seers on the hill, we now know them as Scryers of course and he trusted their visions." Ms. Boson looked around the sitting room and when she was certain that there were no prying eyes or ears close by huddled closer to the girls. Speaking very quietly, Ms. Boson added, "It was recorded that one Scryer was more skilled than the rest and he warned Mandrake that he and all of his men would die if they ventured to the Wastelands. It is also written that this Scryer vowed a life debt if he was wrong. So, Mandrake accepted the offer and decided to bring the Scryer with him. Three days ride from the battlefield, just past the Mother's Scar, the army made camp. Mandrake sent the Scryer along with his two finest scouts to the spy on the battle."

"Why are you whispering so lowly?" asked Cat. "I am whispering, my Lady, because it is not safe to say what I will say too loudly," answered Ms. Boson. Leaning back in toward Cat and Mouse, Ms. Boson continued, "The Scryer and scouts had travelled for two days and were less than a day from the battlefield when they spotted a rider heading toward them. He rode low in the saddle but as he neared their location, the moonlight struck his colors and they made out the Corning crest. He was a messenger from the King and he must be looking for Governor Sorling. The Scryer told the scouts that the messenger could not reach Sorling's camp. The scouts spoke quickly and then one mounted and sped toward the path the messenger was using. Both scout and messenger were out of view beyond a copse of trees but the Scryer could hear one horse rear up and an escalation of voices. Then, silence. Moments later, the scout rode out of the trees and dismounted, waving his hands broadly. The Scryer and the remaining scout brought their horses down to the other scout and what he held in his hands changed Dorias forever."

"What was it? Please tell us. Don't stop now. Please," begged the girls. Ms. Boson readied herself and continued. "Neither Scout could read which was beneficial to the Scryer, as under King Corning's seal was a letter in his own hand. A letter that stated with all certainty that the Dagenskur were poised to enter the fray. The letter commanded Sorling to bring his army to bear in support of the realm. It also demanded penance for his inaction and his failure to arrive as directed weeks earlier. The Scryer wrote on the back of the summons that he would record the battle and then return to Prophet's Call to debrief his liege, King Sorling, and to secure his place by his King's side. He signed his name, Archibald Morecap, Scryer to the King."

Mouse perked up and squealed. "Is he related to Duke Morecap, the Spy Master?" Cat interjected, "Of course he is, why else would Ms. Boson be so secretive." Ms. Boson grinned slightly and said, "Girls, I believe that is about enough with our history for the day. I'm sure the Queen is ready for supper and we shouldn't make her wait." The girls bounded from the sitting room and disappeared through the massive, ornate doors that led to the main hall. Ms. Boson cleaned up the writing supplies and placed the texts on a shelf next to a large book, old and yellowed. Ms. Boson brushed her fingers over the book's spine and pulled it to her. She opened the book and on the first page there was the title 'Lineage of House Sorling, leaders of Tantra'. She pulled her lips into a frown as she thought of how she told her little Princesses mostly truth about how their line ascended the throne. The version where the Governor smartly used the Scryer to take power just as it's written in the pages before her now. What she yearned to tell was the story behind the ruler. The story of how magic ruled the world. She would never do that though. She valued her life too much. She valued her little Princesses who became surrogate daughters after the King died three summers ago and the Queen just after Mouse was born. Yes, she wanted to tell the entire truth, not just the truth found in books.

12

Kahlen forged his path through the woods and moved further south from the Orphans. The forest thinned a bit and the ground softened. Kahlen had spent the better part of the last week trying to convince his new staff to give up his blade, with no effect. He had practiced extensively and felt confident that he could call upon the power within to both light his way and to create fire. Kahlen's confidence grew as for the last two nights he was able to take down a rabbit and then a turkey. The rabbit had been crisped but after cleaning there were only five mouthfuls of food. As for the turkey, the light had blasted the feathers off of the bird and scorched a good portion of it. What he salvaged, Kahlen cooked on a flat stone resting in a strong fire. There was a small cave, more like a rocky overhang with a slight indentation than a cave that Kahlen used for two nights. During that time, Kahlen dried the remaining pieces of turkey and shoved them in his pockets. Kahlen slept fitfully that night and woke to find his staff glowing brightly. Kahlen lay on his left side facing the fire that marked the opening of the tiny cave with his back to the earthen wall. He grasped the staff with his right hand and propped himself up on his left elbow. "What are you doing?" he asked the staff. Kahlen yawned and stretched his neck, and then sat up licking his parched lips and squinted past the staff and into the darkness of night. He strained to stand and walked gingerly past the fire that needed to be stoked back to life. Since he was up, Kahlen decided to relieve himself on the first tree he reached.

After wetting the bark, Kahlen rubbed his eyes and yawned again. He had rested the staff against an adjacent tree, and when he grabbed it to head back to the fire it lit up so brightly that for one hundred feet in every direction night turned to day. The light startled the animals and Kahlen could hear the skittering of claws on bark and the rustling of brush as they scampered away. Kahlen tapped the middle of the staff and held it up to his ear and shook it as if he was knew what he was listening for. Kahlen shrugged his shoulders, and then the hairs on his neck rose as he heard the low grunt behind him. Kahlen swallowed hard, crouched, and turned with the staff pointed ahead of him in a defensive position. Sitting on its hind legs was a bear. No, it was *the* bear. The bear from a couple of weeks ago. Kahlen didn't know how he knew—but he knew. The bear had tracked him all the way from the mountains to this spot. As Kahlen moved, the bear followed him with its eyes and when he stepped backwards the bear rolled forward onto all four paws, raised its head and grunted loudly. Kahlen stopped moving and the bear nodded. He moved one step forward and the bear nodded again. Kahlen jumped backwards and the bear sprung forward and grunted again. Kahlen took a deep breath and said, "I don't know what kind of game you are playing, bear, but you need to go before I strike you down."

Kahlen half expected the bear to answer his challenge and suddenly found the predicament amusing. Kahlen knew that if he had to, he could probably kill the bear in the blink of any eye, but he did not want to. When he looked into the bear's eyes, he could have sworn that there was something special inside. He tried to shoo the bear away. He waved the staff and even yelled as he mocked charged the bear. The bear sat on its haunches and then rolled to its side facing the fire. The bear nosed the rocks ringing the fire pit and went to sleep. Kahlen could not go to sleep. Not with the bear only feet away. Instead, Kahlen foraged for some dry branches and brought a large handful to the fire and placed it in the pit. Kahlen focused the staff on the pile of kindling and brought it to flame. The bear seemed to grumble in an almost appreciative manner. Kahlen backed away slowly and with the light of his staff leading the way, worked his way up past the cave and continued his trek west.

As the sun rose, the bear sniffed the air and nosed the ground where a piece of the dried turkey lay. The bear snapped up the meat and then lumbered westward, grunting and shaking its head. By midday, the bear had picked up Kahlen's scent and had to slow its pace so that it would not overtake the boy. The bear knew where the boy relieved himself and where the boy stopped to eat. The scraps of food left by the boy did not satisfy the bear but it ignored its hunger to follow him. The bear could tell that based on the track the boy was taking, that within the next day he would be faced with the impassable river; The Old Warrior. It would be there, the bear thought, that the boy's fate would be decided. The boy would either choose to go south biding his time until reaching Trader's Bridge to continue westward or to take the East Road toward East Watch and points south, or he could head north which would take him to the Heaven's Crown and Black Lake. The bear pondered the choices a moment and thought, "No, not north. Not yet." The bear, alerted by smoke in the air, grumbled with hunger and decided that maybe it should find out what the boy had caught for food today.

Kahlen clear cut a wide swath of brush and made several small fires in a semi-circle less than ten feet from where he placed a healthy mound of moss, some dry but mostly soft and a little damp. Damp was okay with Kahlen because he'd be off the dirt for a night. He chose an area to camp that gave him a little protection from the wind as there was the husk of an ancient tree that he wedged the moss against. The series of fires he set kept the area so warm that for the first time in weeks, Kahlen fell to sleep thinking of home. Kahlen slept so soundly that he never woke when the staff lit up. He never heard the bear foraging through his pack looking for food. He never heard the bear dig at the ground trying to make a comfortable place to sleep. He never heard the soft moan pass through the bear's lips as it slowly turned into a woman. The bear, now a girl, sat naked tearing through what remained of the food drying on the stone in the middle of the nearest fire. Sated, the girl stood and stretched. Her lithe body glistened with sweat in the light of the fires. The girl grabbed Kahlen's pack and found an old, stained shirt that when on, hung down to her mid-thigh.

The girl reached toward the staff and when she touched it the light went out. The boy grumbled and turned over in his sleep. The girl eyed him, and thought to herself that it is a good thing that the river is close because she didn't need to be a bear to track him the way he smelled. The girl called out abruptly "hey, boy, wake up," and Kahlen smacked his face on the old tree as he tried to catch his bearing. "What, who, who are you? Whaddya want?" he croaked. The girl, unaffected to Kahlen's blurting, raised her right eyebrow and lied. "I'm a traveler heading west and I need your help." Kahlen, his eyes now adjusted to being awake recognized his shirt and exclaimed, "You've stolen my clothes!" The girl, frustrated, responded "no, I didn't. I borrowed your shirt, here take it back." and she proceeded to rip the shirt over her head and tossed it at Kahlen. Kahlen, flummoxed, tried not to stare at the girl who stood defiantly in her altogether without a care, without any shame. Kahlen tried to look away but couldn't. The girl chided Kahlen, "Don't tell me you've never seen a girl before. Now, it gets cold here and I haven't found any clothes since my group was attacked three nights ago." Kahlen handed the girl the shirt and said "here, you can wear it. Why did you get attacked?" The girl pulled the shirt down and sat cross legged facing Kahlen. Kahlen struggled to regain his composure and then looking anywhere but at the girl added "and we need to find you some pants." The girl laughed and then adjusted herself to sit sideways with her knees together and asked, "Better?" Kahlen, relieved, said "yes".

The girl talked for an hour and told of the horrors of coming back from her swim to find her three companions dead and all of their belongings gone. Even the tent was taken so she was left with nothing, no food, no weapons and obviously, no clothes. She told Kahlen that it wasn't safe to only walk along The Old Warrior as bandits and bears were common. She told Kahlen that if they left at dawn they would see the river by mid-day. Kahlen's eyes widened at the news that he was so close to the river. His mind raced with the possibilities. The girl took that moment to set the wheels of fate in motion. "I'm not sure where you are going but if I were you I would not head north cause if the bandits don't get you the tribes from the Roguelands will. They don't let many people get near Black Lake. I think they worship it or something."

Kahlen rubbed his jaw and rolled the staff in his right hand. He used the staff to stand and held his hand out to the girl. The girl tucked her head and frowned at the empty hand and asked, "What are you doing?" Chagrined, Kahlen pulled his hand back and said, "I was going to shake your hand and say you're welcome to join me as far as you'd like or as far as we can get you some real clothes and I can get my shirt back." The girl realized her mistake and shoved her hand out toward Kahlen who took it in his and shook his hand vigorously. "Thank you," she said to Kahlen. Kahlen said, "You're welcome, let's get a head start," and pried his hand from her grip. Kahlen grabbed his pack, slung it over his shoulder and tapped the staff on the ground. The crystal glowed and Kahlen willed the light to spread out to lead their way. The girl stood amazed and looked to Kahlen for some indication as to how he did it. With no answer forthcoming, the girl turned her attention to the path ahead of her. She couldn't help but smell the area, the boy and the hint of the river just hours away. The hard part was over or so she thought. The boy smiled at her, a warm and genuine smile that made her a little uneasy and un-focused. The boy said, "my name is Kahlen Bo...er...just Kahlen. My name is Kahlen what's your name?" The girl did not appear to hear the question and she said "Pardon?" In fact, she had heard but did not know what to say. Where she lived, they didn't use conventional names. Everyone recognized each other by smell. As Kahlen repeated his query, the girl looked around surreptitiously and then spotted something that was familiar. Growing on a tree was a lush green vine that bloomed each spring with the tastiest flowers she'd ever eaten. The traders who visited her village called the vine "Ivy Rose". "My name," she paused, "is Ivy Rose."

13

Yvette Sorling, the "Good" Queen of Tantra, stood in flowing robes of crimson on the stone steps that led from her bedroom to the tower that overlooked the capital city of Corning and for miles in any direction. It has been rumored that on the clearest of days one could see the Gold Sea far off to the west. Yvette had loved coming to these steps, the way the stone arched away from the castle proper and curved gently like an elongated corkscrew reaching through the air until it met the tower entrance some one hundred and fifty feet below. Yvette was adored by her people and her bravery in the face of loss when her father, the King Magnus Sorling V, was found dead in the mud, outside of the stables where he cared for his favorite horse. The shock of his loss was still reverberating throughout the land when Yvette strode into the council chambers, scepter in hand, a retinue of guards at her heel and simply ascended the steps to the throne, sat, and asked plainly "what is on my agenda?" The council murmured among themselves, not truly in discord but certainly surprised as no one could remember there ever being a ruling Queen. Yvette paid very little attention to the majority of the assembled men and instead gazed among those who came to view the proceedings as was the common practice of the time. When the chatter stopped, the chief counsel, Lord Byrr, bowed upon approach to the throne and waited to be recognized. Yvette let him stand there a moment to think about who was in charge and when she was fairly certain that her point was made said ever so politely, "Please, Lord Byrr, you've been so valuable to my father and to my entire family. Do you have anything of import to bring to your Queen, this morning?" Lord Byrr righted himself and slowly raised his eyes to gauge his Queen's approval and when he saw Yvette smile thinly he proceeded, "My, Queen please accept the council's condolences for your great father's passing. On a personal note, your father was not only my King, but my friend as well. I hope to continue aiding you during your...rule." Yvette noticed the way Byrr paused at the end but did not allow herself to worry about this man's misconception. He, like the rest of the council and the Lords and Ladies of Tantra, would come to love her and respect her as their Queen and there would be no pause the next time he addressed her. She was certain of that.

Three hours of debate and pleas from people wronged expecting recompense for some slight real or imagined. Two more hours of discussions regarding taxes and the whispers of revolt from one corner of the land to the other. Finally, one hour of the professional groveling that only a rich man fearing his loss of position, power, or money could present. By the end of her first day of rule, Queen Yvette knew that as long as she wasn't bored to death she could handle these obvious men. What she needed to find out was could she still keep the hearts of the people even while becoming the one true law. Her father had often told her that it was far more important to be respected by her people than loved. Love is fleeting, he would say, but respect is eternal. He would also say that it was easier said than done because the common people would never make it easy. Sure, they would run to her with open arms and declare their love for her but the first time a harvest was short, or if supply lines were interrupted or if Wintersbane came to the border and the men and boys needed to be conscripted, how they would turn. Respect was the key. If, you could maintain the peace and balance the needs of the common folks without elevating expectations, people would be content. If you tried too hard to get them to like you and you kept trying to give and give then they would feel entitled and civil unrest would surely follow when you would inevitably have to take something away. So, he cautioned, that a wise ruler would worry about keeping the people safe and if that ruler made each decision based on that and only that, then no one could argue against the decision. You must be consistent, she could hear him in her mind, and you must be vigilant.

The Good Queen finally found some time to visit some of the merchants whose shops, both permanent and makeshift, lined Protector Road, the avenue closest to the palace, and the first road in the capital ever lined with crushed stone. Originally used by the elite guard units protecting Kings of the past, it is now the only area in the city where common folk and the elite mingle freely. Yvette loved how the area looked and felt like an animal. A breathing beast with so many legs and a strong heartbeat. The clinking of coin and the chatter of barter was like a symphony to her ears. The Queen's guard had been ordered to stay close enough to respond to trouble but not so close as to make her seem unapproachable. As she spied the wares at one stall, she caught the eye of a girl, maybe as old as her baby sister, Mouse, who was playing with a straw doll. Yvette approached and asked the girl, "Sweet? What do you offer here?" The girl smiled and without speaking gently pulled on the pant leg of a man whose back was turned. The man glanced down and shook the girl's hair with his left hand. The little girl was pointing toward the Queen and when the man fully realized he had a customer he smiled broadly and held his hands out to either side. The Queen asked the merchant, "What do you sell?" The man smiled again and removed the canvas covering his supplies. There were several engraved items, including cups and plates. The art on the items was quite good though the metals used were of a soft and poor quality. These pieces could be fine to look at but absolutely unusable. The Queen was about to leave the stall when she caught a glimpse of a beautiful hair pin made from something so black and shiny that the Queen had to hold it. The pin was virtually weightless and was smooth as the finest linens lining her bed. She expected it to be cold to the touch but it was warm. "How much?" she asked the man and he sheepishly shrugged his shoulders and looked to the little girl. The girl was making some kind of shapes with her fingers and the man made a series of shapes back. The little girl spoke, "Da says that he would accept a fair price but would not want to offend such a beautiful lady by bartering." The Queen smiled back and measured the comely features of the tall mute. She imagined him cleaned, dressed with finery and dancing. He would have to be able to dance with a face so strong. "Tell your Da that I prefer to barter, but if he insists, I will simply pay what I think it is worth." The girl relayed the message and the man bowed his head and mouthed thank you. The Queen reached into her small purse and pulled out two golden full pieces, a price more than the merchant could hope to earn in a year. The man spent a moment and stared at the coins and then held both hands to his heart and bowed again. Yvette then snatched one coin and put it back in her purse. Confused and a little sad, the man again used his hands to send a message to the girl. The girl asked Yvette gently, "Has he offended you, Lady?" The Queen shook her head and laughed. "No, dear girl. I have changed the offer. Your father may have the first coin right now, but he must be my guest this evening for dinner and that is when he shall receive the second coin. And, you must attend as well." The girl took some time explaining the offer to her father and with some consternation, he agreed. Yvette said to the girl, "Now, dinner will be in two hours. I would suggest that the two of you accompany me so that you can wash and dress before it is served." The girl said "who will watch our shop, Lady?" Yvette said, "I am sure, little one, that no one would dare steal from you. However, I can place a guard here for the night if that pleases you." The girl smiled. "Yes, thank you, Lady," and grabbed her father's hand. As the trio stepped from the stall, a crimson cloaked guardsman stepped in front of the goods and snapped to attention. The mute looked to his patron and back at the guard and then saw seven more men adorned with the same cloak marching some thirty feet away. The mute grew anxious as this lovely woman headed toward the palace main entrance.

The mute and the girl stopped short of the guard house gate at the base of the path leading to the palace steps while the Lady walked without being stopped. The Lady turned her head over her shoulder and said softly, "Come in please, dinner will be ready soon." The mute and girl smiled at the guards as they passed each one only to be met with a hardened, suspicious glare. The mute and the girl quickened their pace and pulled up just behind the Lady. As they worked up the marble staircase, four large men pulled open gilded doors larger than anything the pair had ever seen or heard of. As they walked in, the mute saw with horror that all who came to the Lady bowed deeply before her. He pulled his hand free from his daughter's and his fingers moved so excitedly that the girl had a hard time understanding him. Eventually, the girl nervously asked the Lady, "Lady, my Da has asked if you are sure that it is okay for us to be here. He worries that the Queen may not approve of a commoner being escorted in like this. My Da, says we should leave before causing you any trouble."

Yvette, put both hands on the girl's face and knelt before her. "My dear," Yvette started, "fear not for the Queen will absolutely adore you and your father. Now head off with these two ladies so that they can ready you for dinner. Oh, and please tell your Da that these ladies here will escort him and ready him for dinner too. Now tell him and scoot off." Yvette kissed the girl on the forehead and stood. The girl explained the words to her father and then skipped off excitedly with the two attendants. The mute, nervous, and unsure walked with trepidation with the attendants waiting for him. Yvette called for her personal staff and four supremely beautiful women and one equally beautiful man rushed to her side and led her to her quarters.

The mute was dazed by his surroundings and by the warmth of the bath. He had never been able to afford a hot bath before. He and his daughter had always taken cold baths in streams or lakes as they travelled. He had rarely even seen soap let alone be covered head to toe in it. One of the attendants scrubbed him with a coarse brush while the other scrubbed his hair with a different soap. The water went black as the caked-on dirt sloughed off his body. So black that one attendant ushered him from the tub and finished cleaning him while he stood on the mosaic tiled floor. Once dried, he had a perfume sprayed over his body and then a man came in with clothes and held a series of outfits up to the mute's body until he was satisfied that he had a fit. Before dressing, the mute was shaved and his hair was cut. An older woman entered with a small animal that the mute had never seen before. The animal looked like a tiny, hairy old man. The mute remained seated and jerked when the animal started picking through his hair. The old woman placed a hand on the mute's shoulders and pushed him back down. The animal continued picking nits and lice from his head until it could find no more. Satisfied that the mute was ready, the old woman took the animal and left. One of the original attendants came back in with the selected clothes including under-clothes. The mute had never worn underclothes as he could never af-ford them but was excited to try them on. The attendant whispered that the Queen would like what she saw from this one and took a horse hair brush from a nearby table and ran it through the mute's hair. The mute closed his eyes and enjoyed the sensation of the bris-tles stroking his hair. The attendant finished and handed the mute the small clothes first and then helped him fasten his pants. He had never seen buttons on pants before. The only pants he'd seen or worn used hemp to cinch it tight.

The mute felt out of place in the fancy clothes but did take a mo-ment to admire his visage in the tall mirror standing near the tub. The door opened and this time his daughter stood there twirling in a little gown looking very much the part of a princess. The mute's heart swelled with pride at his daughter's happiness and he leaned down and kissed her on her painted nose. The girl motioned with her hands and the mute did likewise. They both smiled and the girl hugged him. She said to him "yes, this is the best day of my life, too."

The mute and the girl were led down a series of hallways and then down a spiral staircase before walking through a sheer curtain, soft and slippery to the touch and into a large dining hall that was filling with Lords and Ladies and servants. So many servants were waiting on each person. As the mute and his daughter neared the table they began looking for another table where they would be sitting. They walked toward the back of the hall looking for a servants table or an alcove where common people might sit. Finding no other table, the pair stood silently not knowing what to do. Two girls one about his daughter's age and one old enough to be married approached with welcoming smiles. "Hello, my name is Catherine and this is my sister Rose. She hates that name so we all call her Mouse," said the older girl. The younger girl waved and said "Hello," and took the mute's daughter by the hand and led her toward the table. Catherine walked around the mute and said, "I heard that you are a merchant and that something you've made is the talk of the palace. Please come with me." The mute smiled and took Catherine's extended hand as she led him to a place near the head of the table. The mute smiled at the people who made eye contact with him and then sat down. Catherine took the seat to his left, the chair closest to the large chair that sat empty. The mute's daughter sat directly across from him and was involved in some deep discussion with the little girl who sat in the seat closest to the head.

Wine, bread, salt, and pure butter cream was served to the table. The mute was offered a sampling of it all and he nodded appreciatively at each morsel. He waited to see if others were eating and when he was sure that is was okay to do so, took a bite of bread still warm from the oven. The mute watched his daughter savor everything she tried while the rest of the dinner guests ate and drank with impunity barely even acknowledging the bounty. The mute started thinking about how much of the food he could carry and how many days his daughter could have a full belly instead of going to bed hungry each night.

Catherine attempted to start a conversation with the mute and is wasn't until he put his finger in the air as if asking for a moment's pause and waved to his daughter. The daughter slipped from her chair and was by her father's side listening to his hands. The girl turned to Catherine and explained that her Da was born a mute and also had some trouble hearing. He did not wish to offend the Lady with his silence but could not change his circumstance. Catherine told the girl to apologize for her and mouthed the words "I'm sorry" to the mute. The mute smiled and bowed his head slightly and then held his cup of wine out to her for a toast. They tapped cups and sipped the sweet wine and let their eyes have the conversation their lips could not.

Before the main course was served, the mute saw the guests stand and Catherine waved to grab his attention and then motioned for him to stand. Everyone was looking toward the curtain behind the empty chair and when it parted, the Lady who asked them to dinner was standing there. The mute stole a look to his daughter who stood there, mouth agape. The mute steadied himself with one hand on the back of his chair and the other gently resting on Catherine's shoulder. Catherine did not remove his hand immediately. She let it linger there until her sister, the Queen, approached and arched her brow in an inquisitive manner at the sight. Catherine brushed the mute's hand away and leaned in to hug the Queen. The Queen hugged her back and whispered "That one is mine," and turned to squeeze Mouse's cheek as she stood on the other side of the chair. The Queen asked the crowd "Who's hungry?" She clapped her hands and the feast rolled on.

The mute made eye contact with the Queen and placed both hands on his heart before spreading his arms and mouthing "thank you". The Queen raised her hand to her head where the hairpin was nestled and mouthed "thank you" in return.

The dinner lasted well into the evening and many of the guests had asked for their leave and the Good Queen graciously thanked them and gave them her blessing to do so. A few others lingered in a small group chatting away with an occasional guffaw or snicker to some tasty bit of gossip. Cat had spent the majority of the time looking after Mouse while trying to avoid any contact with the mute. Cat had to fight to not glance at the man and each time her mind drifted to when he placed his hand on her shoulder, a little twinge of excitement coursed through her chest and came to rest in a most embarrassing spot. Cat feared the twinge but didn't shy from it. Flushed with anticipation, Cat stood and kissed her sister, her Queen, on the cheek and asked, "May I be excused, my Queen? I grow tired and I should start getting Mouse to bed as well." The Queen had been spying on the mute who while out of place among the nobles, had such a chiseled look that he would make a fine subject for a statue. The Queen feigned interest in Cat's request and replied dismissively. "Yes, sister. Sleep well," and kissed Cat on her cheek. Cat called to Mouse who pouted for a moment but straightened up in her chair when the Queen snapped her head around and issued a sickly sweet, "Good night, sister."

Mouse smiled nervously and then looked to the mute's daughter. The Queen nodded and Mouse said "come on, you can stay with me in my chambers" and the girl excitedly shared the news with her father, who looked concerned. The mute looked to Cat and Mouse who both nodded expectantly and then to the Queen who mouthed "please". The mute held up his right hand and waved to his daughter and then blew a kiss. The girls all ran off. Mouse and the mute's daughter giggled all the way to Mouse's bed chamber. Once Cat saw both of the girls to bed she made her way to her own bed where she explored those tingles from earlier in the night and she too giggled... multiple times.

The Queen clapped firmly three times and the few remaining diners bowed and made their way out of the hall. The Queen even dismissed her staff for the evening leaving her alone with the mute. The Queen refreshed her cup of wine and then slithered from her chair to claim the one closest to the mute. The mute smiled nervously and then sipped the wine the Queen just poured. The Queen knew the man could not talk and that he could barely hear but felt compelled to talk. With the slightest hint of a purr, the Queen began. "My, my. I can see why my little sister would have such intimate thought about you. Taller than most of my guards, thickly muscled, and with all of that filth removed a face like an angel." The Queen moved from the chair and leaned her lower back against the dining table, her left thigh dangerously close to the mute's own leg. The Queen continued speaking. "I too have much more to show but instead of dirt to remove, I only have this gown. The Queen stepped her left leg over the mute's left leg and slowly lowered herself down until she came to rest just above his knee. Leaning in close to his ear the Queen continued. "I am not as complicated a woman as you'd think. I may live in a palace but I have needs just like any common woman. Needs that must be satisfied. Needs that you must satisfy." The Queen brushed her lips over the mute's ear and he shivered. The Queen darted her tongue over his lobe then down his neck. The mute opened his mouth as if to moan or protest but since his hands lay at his side, the Queen knew there was no protest forthcoming. The Queen became more brazen and writhed slowly while sliding backwards. Her back pressed firmly against the table the Queen reached down and grabbed the hem of her gown. Slowly, in a maneuver well practiced, the Queen pulled the gown over her head leaving her with just a small, silken pair of small clothes, which she used her thumbs to slide down her legs and over her feet. The Queen bit on her finger and arched herself onto the table, knocking dishes aside and spilling wine. She beckoned the mute to her with a curl of her index finger and the mute did as she commanded.

The morning came faster than the Queen expected and was not quite finished with another round with the mute when her attendants arrived to prepare her for the day. Instead of stopping, the Queen made the staff wait and watch until she had one more reply from the mute. Sated, the Queen stood and told her team to wash the mute and the bedding. She wished to bathe before breakfast. Once bathed and dressed, the Queen brought in one of her father's old advisers and ate sugared bread with cream while he explained a matter of importance to one faction or another. By his tone, this man had a personal stake in the matter, the Queen thought. The Queen wanted to be anywhere but here in the palace handling such minute issues. She wanted to be outside, she wanted her people to see her and support her. She had heard the whispers in the palace about the council sending notice to the Governors that Tantra needed a King to rule and wanted the most eligible noblemen to court the Queen. The only way she could stay in power was to be the people's choice. It was a tactical ploy and it may countermand her father's teaching but right now she did not know if she had the time to earn the people's respect.

The Queen called for her guard and said, "I want to walk with my people today. Prepare to leave in fifteen minutes." The commanding guard saluted and led his men out of the palace to wait for his Queen. The Queen sent one attendant to fetch her sisters and moments later Cat, Mouse, and the mute's girl were at her side. "I'm going for a long walk and need you both to be here to receive any visitors. I will return before dinner. I have decided that this one, as the Queen pointed at the mute's daughter, will stay with us for the time being. Bring her to your studies and have her tell her father thank you for being such a wonderful conversationalist after dinner." Cat's eyes fell at the words and knew the Queen found her fledgling desires amusing. Cat bowed her head and said "yes, sis...my Queen". The Queen left the room to go for her walk. Cat turned to mouse and said, "Let's go find Ms. Boson." Then seeing the three quarters of a loaf of sugared bread on the table, she said, "But first..." Cat paused, and the girls each eat a mouthful of the treat right from the Queen's own plate before finding searching out the tutor.

After a tedious session spent mostly teaching the mute's daughter, a girl whose first name was finally determined to be Torrie but shrugged when probed about her last name, about letters and numbers, the three girls walked the spacious palace halls until they reached the chamber where the mute was supposed to be. The room stood empty and there was no sign of the mute. The girls kept searching, turning it into a bit of a game until one of the Queen attendants asked them what they were up to. After a quick recap, during which Torrie told the assembled group her father's name; Raleigh, the attendant told them how she saw firsthand this morning that the man spent the night with the Queen in her own chamber. Mouse found the news exciting. Torrie went crimson of the thought of her father doing, well, something with a woman, let alone the Queen. Cat, her mood soured, found it all to be unbecoming. The fact that her sister actually had the man that she herself had spent the early morning hours pretending to have caused her to curse her sister under her breath. It was then, standing there in front of two snickering girls that Cat realized she was more a woman than a girl. And when you are a woman, you stop playing little girl's games and play games of the heart instead. Cat knew that she would have to become more like Yvette if she was to claim what she desired. Cat thought, I am ready.

The Queen had spent the late morning hours among the people and for the most part found herself well received. She wanted to be more available but with so many people she found herself having difficulty discerning whose concerns should be acknowledged first. Growing hungry, the Queen bade her guard to escort her back to the palace where lunch awaited. A different kind of hunger began to grow within the Queen and she smiled devilishly at the thoughts of the mute and his quiet, gifted tongue. As she walked onto Protector Road, the Queen glanced at the stall where she met the mute and saw it empty. The guard was not there either. The Queen looked to her guard's commander and asked as to the whereabouts of the guard. The commander said his man came back to the barracks this morning after the merchant returned to secure his goods. The Queen asked the commander, "Did the merchant leave the city?" The commander shrugged while saying, "I'm not sure, my Queen, I would not think he'd leave his daughter. He may have already returned to the palace." The Queen's lip quivered and the left corner of her mouth peeled up in a subtle sneer. "Of course, his daughter," she echoed.

14

Ivy always came back with game. She had no weapon, she barely had clothes save for Kahlen's old shirt but she always caught food. This morning was more impressive than the prior eight days combined. A boar, fully tusked, was brought down by Ivy with little more than her hands and determination. Kahlen heard the squeal and by the time he raced through the woods and reached Ivy, the boar was already being dressed. Innards were piled to the side as Ivy reached in and pulled out the inedible parts. Kahlen, worried that the kill would attract other predators, used his staff to scorch the pile of guts to ash. Kahlen. Ivy grabbed a thick branch and slid the branch down the boar's mouth. Ivy then wrapped a piece of cloth around the boar's feet to secure the body to the branch. Cloth, Kahlen noted, that used to be the sleeves of his old shirt. Kahlen was surprised at how heavy the boar was even after the gutting. An animal this big would have fed all of Crescent Bay for a night. Ivy started to hum and the song reminded Kahlen of the wind whipping near the Orphans. They carried the beast back to camp and finished preparing it. Ivy did not want Kahlen to use his magic light to cook today. Instead, she built two fires, one she mounted the majority of the boar over, still tied to the branch which was supported on each end by a brace of crossed pieces of wood tied together by vines. The fire spat and hissed whenever fat from the boar dripped into it and Kahlen's stomach growled in concert.

The second, smaller fire was used to dry out small strips of the boar. Ivy used a flat stone for smaller pieces to crisp them and had two sticks tied like braces, holding the boar angled over the fire. This brace had long, thick pieces draped over it drying slowly amid the heat and smoke from below. Thirsty, Kahlen decided to take his turn on the short walk to the river. The pair had been smart to avoid the river for the most part aside from one bath since their unexpected meeting a few days earlier. However, after wrestling with the decision to head south, it was decided that they had to at least venture to North Watch, which meant crossing Trader's Bridge and possibly encountering Kahlen's past. The bridge was in sight which meant that they were mere hours from the town. Kahlen hoped to trade the boar meat for a knife. The sun moved overhead which meant the boar had been cooking for about five hours. Kahlen placed the dried bits into his pack and cinched it tight. The pack secured over his shoulder, Kahlen grabbed one end of the mounted boar while Ivy grabbed the other. Kahlen expected to carry the majority of the load but Ivy proved to be much stronger than she appeared. She effortlessly pulled her end to her shoulder and mocked Kahlen. "Boy, I'd say you lift like a girl, but you're not that strong. Hey, don't forget your shiny stick." Kahlen crouched for the staff and Ivy followed his movement thinking all the while that the boy was handsome. Ivy cocked her head a bit to the side admiring Kahlen's muscular frame and appreciating it for the first time, then let out a little laugh that gave Kahlen a moment's pause. "What's so funny?" he called back to Ivy. Ivy righted herself and said "nothing, boy, get going before we lose the day," all while thinking that maybe she should have borrowed his pants instead of his shirt. Ivy found herself smiling all the way to town.

Ivy could smell the city miles earlier but as they neared, her senses were accosted. She could smell the wonders from the bakery and the succulent vapors from the smoke house. She could also smell the vermin and waste that lined the shallow gutters that ran from the heart of the city to a man-made aqueduct that must have led to the river just south of Trader's Bridge. Ivy struggled to stay on task as Kahlen led her down a series of narrow streets that twisted like roots from a tree. Ivy was certain that she could never be happy among so many...people. It seemed that no one was happy. Everyone yelled at everyone else. Sometimes she could hear people laughing while they yelled and then peculiarly the people being yelled at would also yell back while laughing. Ivy thought maybe they were all losing their hearing or going mad.

Kahlen stopped outside of the butcher's shop where the butcher quickly waved them away and offered his own brand of colorful language, expertly practiced it seemed, as to where they could place it. Apparently, the butcher only has use for uncooked meat. Ivy lost count of the number of places Kahlen was turned away from and she started thinking that maybe she should just turn into the bear and eat the damn thing. On another street that looked just like the last twenty or so and smelled equally rotten, a bold woman standing in a doorway called out to Kahlen. The woman, wearing less fabric than Ivy sauntered over and propositioned Kahlen. Kahlen stumbled over his words and started apologizing. Ivy was amused to hear Kahlen apologizing for apologizing in the first place. The boy confounded Ivy. He was built like a man. Had the face of one too. He even acted bravely or more so foolishly by travelling the dark woods all the way to the Orphans. Yet, here, in front of this prostitute, this man had turned to a babbling idiot. Snickering, Ivy called to the woman. "Hey," she said, and promptly lifted the tail of what was left of Kahlen's old shirt revealing all to any who cared to look. She proclaimed "he's got enough trouble taking care of this one let alone trying out another." The woman guffawed at the ribald display and even snorted as she backed away. "You know," the woman started, "you ever need work, the boys and the girls would pay plenty to sample your wares."

Kahlen stood dumbfounded. He was not the most talkative man to walk Dorias but knew his way around a conversation. Here, in this little alley, he was as dumb as Old' Gruff, the man kicked in the head by a spooked mare while shoeing the damn thing. Old' Gruff used to travel the roads from Corning to Crescent Bay and he was a fine blacksmith in his youth. As he aged, Old' Gruff visited less often and completed fewer jobs while demanding more money. Kahlen tried to remember if he had had his eighth or ninth name day when the horse reared and came down so hard that Old' Gruff's head went lopsided where the hoof struck him. For three years, Old' Gruff was nursed and when he could be moved, two from the town propped him into his cart and with one driving his cart and the other following with a covered cart of his own, brought him home. In the months leading up to taking Old' Gruff home, Kahlen had often visited and tried to talk to the man. Old' Gruff could not talk very well. What came out was mostly gibberish and drool. Lots of drool. Kahlen always thought that there were words just waiting to explode from Old' Gruff. He swore to any who would listen that Old' Gruff had something to say but just couldn't make the words work. Kahlen wondered if Old' Gruff ever got the words to come out.

Kahlen had not looked back in time toward Ivy to catch the show that the woman was cackling about. He stared at Ivy with hint of envy for what he missed half a beat too long, and Ivy crinkled up her nose and teased "show's over, boy." As Ivy passed the woman they nodded at each other with wily smiles and the woman said "try over at Marco's place. His is the big white building up at the next corner." Ivy thanked the woman and tossed two choice pieces of dried meat to her.

Ahead, they came to the large white building. Ivy had not seen a painted building before and marveled at how clean it appeared. All around lay filth and mud, yet these walls and the front door were unmarked. Hanging from a banister some ten feet overhead were baskets of flowers in bloom. Kahlen knocked on the door and when it opened a man in white cloth wearing so much jewelry that he chimed as he moved stood perplexed. The man said, "May I help you?" He stepped back at the sight of the boar. "My name is Kahlen," Kahlen probed, "and my friend is called Ivy." Ivy didn't wait for Kahlen to bumble this up so she interjected. "We have travelled far and faced many challenges. We are in need of shelter and clothing and would like to offer this pig in trade."

"I see," said the bejeweled man. The man ushered them inside and called for a servant.

The interior of the white building was filled with colored light. A balcony ringed the main room and there were all manner of guests milling about. Directly overhead was etched glass, a depiction of some great war painted in bright colors that diffused the afternoon sun. A squat and portly man stepped heavily down one of two wide staircases in the back of the room that connected the balcony level to the main floor. An audible groan, either from the steps or the man himself, accompanied each labored step. As he neared the end of the stairs, two men, gaunt and dark skinned, wearing bright white pants and adorned with the same jingling bangles as seen on the man who escorted them into the building knelt in fealty. Ivy whispered to Kahlen, "Is he a King?" to which Kahlen replied "I don't know." The floor moved, vibrations deepening as the man drew closer and then he smiled. It was difficult to keep eye contact with the man as what teeth he still had were of gold. The man laughed raggedly and then wheezed and coughed, droplets of sweat beading upon his brow and rolling down his puffy cheeks. "What a gift you have brought me, my God," the man croaked while he tried to catch his breath.

The man stepped right past Ivy and Kahlen and toward the giant boar and clasped his hands before him while taking in the sight. The man cleared the spit from his throat and roared his approval. "It must have weighed several hundred pounds before you took out the tastiest parts. The rest of the meat looks well cared for." In a well-practiced move the man pulled a fist sized chunk from the boar's shoulder and indulged himself with several uninterrupted bites. The man hummed as he chewed and after a moment turned to Ivy and Kahlen. The man nodded and smiled and called out to six of his servants who approached the pig and struggled to move it into the kitchen to prepare for the evening's meal.

The man introduced himself as Marcos Roan, the master of acquisitions for North Watch. Marcos sat down to a glass of sparkling water that he claimed came from the heart of Black Lake itself. Marcos made a point of calling out all of his possessions including his favorite servants. He explained over the course of an hour how nothing happened in this part of the world without him having a piece of it. He even made the boisterous claim that he was the closest thing to royalty this part of Tantra would ever see. Ivy noted that Marcos never seemed to tire of talking about himself and thought that it might be useful information. Marcos did relent just before dinner was served and asked Kahlen why he chose to bring such a tribute to his door this day. Kahlen said he was hoping to trade the boar for clothes for both he and Ivy. It was then that Marcos realized that the woman wore only a long shirt. Marcos frowned and directed two female servants to take Ivy to the bath and to find suitable clothing for a woman. Marcos looked sternly at Kahlen and asked, "Why would you let your woman dress so?" Kahlen replied, "That woman caught and killed the boar with her bare hands. So who am I to argue with her about fashion? Since we are headed north, we did hope to find suitable clothes for that part of our journey. I think she would want pants at least by then." The two men shared a laugh and then Marcos interjected. "My friend, I am not sure when you bathed last but please," and proceeded to call over two new female servants and instructed them to see Kahlen to a bath and scenting.

Kahlen was ushered upstairs and his clothing was peeled from his body by the two servants who exchanged knowing glances even while holding their breath to keep from smelling him. Kahlen stepped over the side of the large tub and into the hot water. Kahlen sank to his shoulders as he sat and watched the two servants sprinkle salts and flower petals and something that smelled sickly sweet that was poured in. One of the servants took a large wooden paddle and started churning the water. As she churned, bubbles appeared all around Kahlen and he stared in amazement as they blossomed around him. He was so caught up in the moment that he did not hear the other woman join him in the bath until she poured fresh water over his head and began working her hands through the tangled mess. The scent of flowers was even stronger now that there were bubbles in his hair and on his face too. The other woman had stopped churning the water and now was also in the tub, but this time she held two large white sponges that she squeezed and more bubbles oozed through her fingers and into the tub. "You are very dirty and must be cleaned," said one servant, and the other added "we must make sure you are scrubbed completely." Kahlen closed his eyes and tried to think of Danielle but the harder he tried to envision her the blurrier his memory became. Finally, he fought through his memory and saw her in the distance staring at the ocean. In his mind he ran toward her, tried to call out to her but no sound would come out. Exhausted, he stopped running some ten feet from her and as his approach slowed, she turned, only instead of Danielle smiling at him it was Ivy. Kahlen woke with a start to find himself atop a soft feather bed in a room filled with flickering light from the dozens of candles set out. Sitting up, Kahlen could hear quite the lively gathering downstairs. Kahlen stood up and looked directly into the tallest mirror he had ever seen. His entire body could fit in the mirror and he took a moment to appreciate the fine soft cloth that covered him. He did not recognize himself and saw that his hair was no longer hanging over his shoulder. It was shaved over both ears and very short in the back. Long on top and piled to the side where the longest strands brushed his forehead just over his left eye. Kahlen looked the stranger in the eye and smiled. "A new look for a new journey," he smirked. Kahlen left the room and headed toward the sounds of revelry.

In the main hall, Marcos was entertaining some fifty people to some outlandish story that involved spiked fruit from the Tropics and one of his former wives. "Ah, he lives after all," cried out Marcos as Kahlen entered the hall. There were several comments, most of them lewd and all of them from the female guests as Kahlen thanked Marcos for his hospitality and found a seat. Kahlen's eyes scanned the table until he came upon Ivy who sat with a bemused look and who stared at him from over her cup of wine. Kahlen mouthed "hi" and Ivy scrunched up her nose and mouthed "who are you?" Kahlen felt his face go flush and his heart began pounding as he watched Ivy savor the wine. Kahlen fought the urge to just call out Ivy's name and instead averted his gaze aside and focused on the choices of food and drink before him. Kahlen ate with a voracious fervor that still did not sate him. A second cup of wine begat a third and it continued throughout the night. Every time Kahlen paused his mind turned to Ivy and every time he glanced her way, there she was smiling at him.

When dinner ended, some less hearty guests made their way home while most stayed to sing and dance or to pursue some other desire. Some guests made their way to upstairs rooms and some just made their intentions known right there in the hall. There was no shame in any of the activities. No one paid much attention to anyone else and everyone was accepted openly. Kahlen found himself in alternating conversations with men and women in various states of undress but found him looking for Ivy most of the time. He didn't think he was being obvious but Marcos slapped him firmly upon his back and said "don't waste your time waiting for one flower to bloom when the fields grow wild with them and they are waiting to be picked." Marcos laughed at his own joke and walked toward a welcoming husband and wife who beckoned him to join them on the couch. Kahlen stepped in and around the pleasure seeking couples and made his way upstairs. Kahlen walked past his room and went to Ivy's room. He was about to knock upon her door when he heard the unmistakable sounds of passion echo from within. Disheartened, Kahlen stepped back from her door and retraced his steps toward his own door. He beat himself up internally for having such foolish thoughts. He didn't even know this girl. Not really. He didn't even trust her fully. She was just some strange girl he caught stealing his shirt and he was just lonely from the past few months since his banishment. She was nothing to him yet he had dreamed of her and her face is the one he saw when he tried to think of his first love, Danielle. He steeled himself with the thought that it was a combination of being tired and too much wine that caused him to have these feelings. Kahlen gave one last look toward Ivy's door as he heard a loud punctuation to the night moves going on somewhere inside.

Kahlen, more frustrated for having feeling for someone he didn't know opened the door to his room to find clothes on the floor leading to his bed sheer Ivy sat in profile, the silky sheets pulled up to her shoulders. Kahlen's tongue couldn't form the words his brain worked so hard to come up with. He just stood and stared. Kahlen's eyes widened further as Ivy dropped the sheet and lay back upon the stacked pillows at the head of the bed. "Someone claimed my room so I was hoping you wouldn't mind..." Kahlen swallowed and shook his head slowly from side to side. Ivy propped herself up on both elbows wand with a wicked upturn of her upper lip said, "Boy, this is the part where you take your clothes off and show me what you've got." Kahlen nodded silently and grinned in a way that gave Ivy chills. Kahlen disrobed and Ivy pulled forward onto all fours as he closed. Ivy looked up into Kahlen's eyes and said "you smell too clean. Let's see if we can dirty you up a bit." She lunged up to grab Kahlen about his neck and kissed him deeply. Ivy pulled Kahlen to the bed and it wasn't until late in the morning that she let go.

Kahlen and Ivy dressed and made their way to the main hall where there were no signs of last night's party. Only a few servants were visible and there was a small basket of fruits and cheeses left out with a bottle of the sparkling water Marcos loved. Ivy and Kahlen ate silently while brushing their hands together and entwining their legs.

One servant came forward with a chest. Within the chest were four outfits. Two for each Ivy and Kahlen. One was of soft leather and it was padded like the bed they shared the other was rugged and had three layers of leather with a metal mesh interwoven between. Under the mesh was three inches of woven fur that would help keep the cold out. Two cloaks lay at the bottom of the chest. The cloaks were heavy and soft. They were dyed bright white like the soft clothes they wore now. Another servant brought up a new empty pack that had two thick straps of leather on the back that allowed the wearer to slide both arms through and carry the pack securely upon their back. Ivy claimed the pack and without a care, stripped from the soft clothes and put on the padded leather outfit. She stuffed a cloak, the armor and the soft clothes into the pack and put it back on her back. "This is wonderful; I barely even notice it at all. I feel like I could carry the world in this." Kahlen had followed Ivy's lead and dressed in the padded leather while placing his own cloak, armor and soft clothes within his pack which he pulled over his left shoulder. "My staff?" he asked the nearest servant. The servant backed away without a word and returned with Kahlen's staff. The servant also had his old clothes, which Kahlen first thought of waving off but upon reflection chose to accept and shoved them into his pack. "Thank you for cleaning them," he told the servant who simply bowed her head. A second servant stepped to Ivy and held out the tattered shirt she had worn for the past few weeks and she happily accepted it, and after thanking the servant pulled the shirt to her face and inhaled deeply. Kahlen thought it odd but Ivy added, "I can still smell you...and me. I like that." Kahlen smiled and said, "Well, we won't smell like flowers once we hit the road." Ivy stopped him and said "no, not like flowers. Like a man and a woman. Like the day we met."

Kahlen asked if Marcos would see them off but the servant simply shook his head, and then one of the jeweled men led them to the door and opened it with a deep bow. No one said goodbye to them, but it was a beautiful day and they both felt ready for any challenge.

From his window, one floor above the balcony level, Marcos watched Ivy and Kahlen walk out of view and then turned to the scryer who sat at a small table next to Marcos' bed. From the scrying stone, Marcos could see Duke Morecap, who thanked him for his service. Marcos gave a detailed report of the night's activities including the coupling of Ivy and Kahlen. The Duke's image shimmered like the painted glass upon Marcos' ceiling. "Very good news, Marcos. The boy is headed north correct?" "Yes, Duke," Marcos responded. "And, the way to the forgotten pass?" This time the scryer answered. "It is made ready." "Excellent. I'll make a hero out of him, yet."

The Scryer stood after the Duke's image disappeared and collected the stones which he placed into individual slots within a fabric pouch. The Scryer presented a second pouch from within his robes and handed it to Marcos. Marcos jostled it in his hands and heard the song of coins that he coveted. The Scryer exited the room and Marcos felt the weight of the coins for a moment, and then turned the pouch over and poured the contents onto his bed. Marcos grinned at the glittering gold and picked one of the coins up and rolled it between his fingers. He stopped the coin between his thumb and fore finger of his right hand. On the side facing him was the familiar seal of Tantra and when he flipped the coin over the face staring back was neither of the dead King nor of the new Queen. It was the face of Duke Morecap. Marcos was staring not at wealth but at treason. Marcos grabbed the coins and stuffed them back into the pouch and then frantically scanned the room for a place to hide the coins. Marcos collected himself and slid his bed aside, exposing an edge of well-worn carpet. Marcos flipped up the carpet and then ran his hands over the floor boards until he found the loose one. Marcos pushed on one end of the board until the other end popped up. Marcos removed the board, pulled out a leather satchel wrapped in brown cloth and put the coin purse into the satchel. He wrapped the satchel back in the brown cloth and dropped it inside the floor. Marcos popped the board back into place and covered it up with the rug and pushed his bed back into its original position. Satisfied that no one would know about his hiding place, he called for his servants to start his bath water. Marcos walked slowly to his window and sucked in his breath as he saw the Scryer standing on the road in front of his house with his finger held before his lips as if to say "hush". Marcos mimicked the Scryer and the Scryer smiled, bowed, and walked away. Marcos called for wine and headed to his bath.

15

Prophet's Call had long been Tantra's spiritual center and over the centuries it had morphed into the nation's mystical center as well. It was here, in the Crystal Citadel, where Duke Morecap continued his forefather's legacy. It was here that he first was handed down the unedited battlefield account that detailed how the War for Dorias, as it has come to be known, truly concluded. A war that had been prophesized decades earlier as part of a series of prophecies that continued through the modern day. Duke Morecap believed in modern prophecy ever since his grandfather's vision came true. Thirty one years earlier, some five years before the Duke's birth, his grandfather saw that his son would be struck down in his sleep on the eve of a Queen's birth. He also saw that his son's son would be birthed in flame, shadows, and secrecy. The vision was captured on the pages of the scribe's "Book of Dreams" which chronicled the visions of the Precept of the Order of Scryers. Since the War for Dorias, the Precept had been a descendant of the Morecap line and as one would expect, many of the visions were simple things that benefited the family. If one spent much time reading them as Duke Morecap had, one would see that some "visions" were no more than premeditated actions disguised as prophecy. At its heart, the book was a poorly disguised bit of subterfuge, but few would take the time to read it and none would dare argue with the accuracy.

The Duke's Grandfather predicted quite accurately the events surrounding the Duke's birth. On the eve of Queen Yvette's birth, the Duke's father was found dead, draped over the edge of his bed, a slender blade lodged just under his left arm pit. Just across Protector's Road a fire raged in the noble's district. Within the inferno, one building stayed unbent. All around the Scryer's station chaos and confusion spread as fast as the flames.

It took well into the evening before the fire was brought low by the water brigade and as some milled about, either exhausted from fighting the fire or from gawking at it, a muffled cry was heard coming from the Scryer's station. One person risked injury by pulling the charred timber from a neighboring building away from the station's door. When the door was opened, a baby was found, wrapped in the finest linen was eagerly feeding from the bosom of a beautiful woman who was wearing a heavy cloak. The first man to enter recognized Lady Tabitha, King Sorling's sister and a royal who had been missing from court for several months. The man asked Lady Tabitha if he could offer her any assistance and she directed him to fetch the Precept. It was not long before the Precept arrived and as he walked toward the station door Lady Tabitha exited, cooing to the newborn. The wind blew a heavy curtain of smoke down the row partially obscuring her and the babe until she held the baby out to the Precept. "Your Grandson, Precept," was all Lady Tabitha said as she handed the child to the Precept and then turned away without word and walked into the gutted district.

"So, have all of your Grandfather's visions come true?" asked Danielle with a rush. The Duke sat on the edge of the ornate bed, one hand reaching to pull on his slippers, the other being tugged to Danielle's lips. A look of exasperation faded as the Duke felt Danielle's kisses upon his hand. "Don't you have a little more time for me?" she added between each soft kiss. The Duke leaned his tall frame over her and kissed her warmly. He paused as if remembering something distant in his mind and then let the kiss go. "I must leave Prophet's Call for a short while," said the Duke matter-of-factly. The Duke kissed Danielle upon her forehead and wordlessly left the chambers. Danielle slid from the bed without securing her simple sheer robe and opened the balcony door. Danielle let the cool, early morning air dance over her skin and walked to the railing. Below, a retinue of soldiers stood at attention and they snapped their boots together and saluted the Duke as he climbed aboard the closest carriage. She could see little specks of light, fire pits most likely, dotted throughout the hill side far beyond the soldiers who now turned in unison and began quick marching behind the Duke. When she looked skyward the stars looked the reflection of the fires. A quick flash of fire traced through the night sky and she remembered the first time she watched a star fall; the day she met Duke Morecap.

• • •

Danielle was all of thirteen when she bled for the first time. The nurse in Crescent Bay informed the Dock Master that his daughter was a "woman" now and that she would be able to carry the family line when a "suitable" partner was chosen. At the time, most in the village were not up to speed with the plan for Kahlen Bowsprit and the nurse made her wry comment with the notion that everyone knew that Danielle and Kahlen would end up together. A handful of days after her bleeding, Danielle was instructed to travel to North Watch with her father and a three cart caravan of goods to trade at market.

The horses made fair time on the Northern Trail and they soon passed over the wide, rough waters of the Old Warrior by way of the Trader's Bridge. The bridge was the largest structure in northern Tantra and Danielle felt like she needed to hold her breath for fear that her nerves would shake the bridge through its foundation and bring it crashing to the ground. As the caravan crept over the center of the bridge and started moving closer to North Watch, Danielle forgot about the bridge and clasped her hands over her mouth to mute a squeal of delight. She had never seen a city so vast. She could only imagine the wonders within the rows of buildings. The buildings seemed to be two or three times taller than her home. Black and gray smoke belched from rooftops and as they neared, a slight film of soot seemed to coat her skin and clothing. The Dock Master had been explaining something of importance to her but Danielle heard not a word. Danielle had been wearing a hat to shade from the sun but here in between the buildings there was little sunlight, so she untied the hat from beneath her chin and then released the pin holding her hair up letting it flow over her shoulders. Danielle stepped down from the cart and patted the two horses that pulled her all this way. Danielle went to the back of the cart and found the feedbags for the horses, tied them on and left the horses to check on the other two carts. Danielle fed the other two pair of horses and then climbed back into her cart to wait for her father.

The Dock Master returned to Danielle and began untying the feedbags from the horses. "Smart girl. Thank you," said Danielle's father. When all of the horses were readied, the Dock Master snapped them into action and he patted Danielle on her knee to get her attention. "Yes, father?" Danielle asked. "We can't trade without a permit. New law imposed by the Queen," answered the Dock Master. "So, what do we do?" Danielle asked in a worried tone. "We, my little one, have to get a permit from the constable," replied her father easily. "Then," the Dock Master continued, "We will trade away and maybe find you a new dress. One fit for a woman grown." Danielle hugged her father tightly and began listing all the types of fabrics or designs she's ever heard of while they slowly passed from one line to the next until they reached the guardhouse.

At the gate, the Dock Master explained why they were here, and after allowing the guards to inspect the goods, with a fair amount of sampling to boot, were allowed to enter the Constable's grounds. The group was commanded to stay with their goods while a runner went in to speak with the Constable. Twenty minutes later, the wide doors opened and the town Constable, a rotund, hairy faced ogre of a man lumbered menacingly toward them. Before the door shut, another man, tall, slender, and very handsome walked to the porch, and Danielle could not take her eyes off of him. Danielle was startled from her trance-like state as the Dock Master bellowed "this is outrageous" to the Constable who looked as if he needed to wipe food from his chin. As the debate raged, the tall man from the porch sauntered toward the action. He moved quite gracefully for a man so tall. Not gangly like one would expect. As he came closer, Danielle noticed that his face was a bit angular but still strikingly handsome. He carried himself with that of someone with power and influence. He bowed his head slightly toward Danielle while smiling pleasantly and gave her but the quickest of winks before moving around the front of the cart to see what all the fuss was about.

The moment the Dock Master saw the tall man he fell silent and bowed his eyes to the ground. The tall man grinned and vigorously shook the Dock Master at the shoulders. "Constable Graves meet Dock Master Averill of Crescent's Bay," the tall man let the statement linger in the air for a moment until the Constable started nodding his head while saying "yes, yes, of course, Crescent Bay, please excuse me." The Constable moved as quickly as his trunk like legs would allow and disappeared through the doors. The tall man moved past the Dock Master and held his handout to Danielle and said, "Is this? Can it be? Danielle? My, you have become a most fetching woman." Danielle looked to her father who mouthed "take his hand" and she did so while stepping down from the cart. The tall man blurted out. "The last time I saw you was ten years past I think. Isn't that right Averill?" The Dock Master replied weakly "yes, Duke, I believe it was." Danielle blinked and then looked intently at the tall man. Danielle brazenly asked "are you really a Duke?" To which the Duke smiled and bowed with a flourish while acknowledging that he was, indeed, a Duke. The Dock Master glared at his daughter in a failed attempt to get her to stop asking questions but Danielle continued. "I've heard of the Governors and the Royal family of course but what dies a Duke do? Are there a lot of Dukes? I can tell you are powerful as the Constable went scurrying off after you just glanced at him."

The Duke took Danielle's arm in his and said to the Dock Master, "the Constable will be back out with your special permit as agreed upon and you will find that there will be quite more for you to bring back, so he is procuring three new carts and drivers as the trading season will be quite favorable to you, my friend." "Thank you, Duke Morecap," stammered the Dock Master. The Duke asked Danielle if she makes it to the city often and she said that it was her first time since being a baby. Danielle excitedly told the Duke how this was a special trip since was declared a woman and that she could now be a part of caravan. The Duke stepped back and eyed Danielle and said, "But if you are a woman grown, then you must start dressing like one." Danielle giggled and mentioned how her father had just surprised her with the promise of a new dress to celebrate her new place.

The Duke said, "Averill, I have a splendid idea. While you and your group finish your very successful trading session, I will show Danielle to the dressmaker and show her some of the finest shops the city has to offer. I will make arrangements for you to stay here for the evening, take advantage of the baths and sleeping quarters and we will meet back for a late supper as my personal guests. No request will be denied. As you know, I am a man of my word am I not?" The Dock Master replied, "You are indeed, Duke Morecap. Thank you." The Dock Master watched as his daughter and the Duke walked arm in arm toward the Duke's carriage only to be interrupted by the clammy hand of Constable Graves patting him on the back. The Constable handed an official trading writ with his seal and then whispered to the Dock Master that the traders would be coming to him with six cart loads of goods—far superior to anything they had ever traded for before and that his home was theirs whenever they visited. The Constable called for three of his guards to stand watch over the carts and invited the weary travelers inside his home all the while apologizing for not knowing who they were. It seemed that the Constable was new and had not been apprised of the arrangement between Crescent Bay and the Duke, and the Constable was hell-bent on ensuring there would be no complaints today or any day moving forward.

· · ·

Danielle moved back into the Duke's chambers from the balcony and tied her robe at the waist. She added two small logs to the fire crackling within the fireplace and stirred the embers with a wrought iron poker. The fresh logs hissed as the flames drew breath and licked the untouched bark. Danielle knelt on the plush rug and embraced the warmth of the fire. Bored, Danielle arose and stepped quickly over the cold marble floor until she came to the Duke's private library. Standing before the voluminous tomes, she traced her finger over the spines of several works until she found one titled "Death on the Green Sea" by a man named Raynor Talbot and pulled it from the shelf. Danielle carried the book back to the rug in front of the fireplace and began to read. After tearing through the first several pages, Danielle held the book against her chest and her thoughts drifted back to that day in North Watch.

· · ·

Walking with the Duke, Danielle found each new shop more exciting than the last and each new person met more exotic than the last. Danielle may have been declared a woman grown but she could not help but act like a girl for much of the day until she turned the corner and faced the entrance for a dressmaker. In the large window front, there were two dresses, more beautiful than anything Danielle had ever seen. The Duke settled just beside Danielle and rested his hand on hers giving it a warm squeeze. The Duke opened the door and ushered Danielle in. Inside the shop, he spoke quietly to the proprietor and a sudden flurry of activity warped around Danielle. Two or three women and another man had appeared from somewhere in the recesses of the building and they were all talking rapidly and moving her arms and legs, taking measurements and holding different fabrics up against her skin. The workers seemed to be arguing about something that Danielle just could not decipher. After conferring with the Duke and coming to an apparent agreement, the two women brought out a large barrier that unfolded and was used to block the view of the men in the shop as she stripped down to her under clothes. One of the women assistants shook her head and motioned for Danielle to remove it all. Danielle did as the women bade and stood there knowing that a strange woman was turning her about while she was nude and accepted that this must be what a woman does. Especially a woman getting a new dress. She relaxed slightly and as the woman turned her to her right, marking her thigh with a wax pencil. Danielle could see her profile in a tall mirror just outside the barrier. The woman who stared back from the mirror was taller than she imagined and her breasts were larger and firmer than she expected. The slimness of her waist accentuated the curve of her bottom and her legs looked toned and long. As the assistant turned her again Danielle look headlong unto the woman in the mirror and smiled. The nurse didn't need to tell her she was a woman. One look was all she needed. As she was about to be turned again, Danielle saw the woman in the mirror but this time she also saw the image of Duke Morecap smiling. At first, Danielle felt heat grow inside her and blushed. When she faced away from the mirror she tried to peek over her shoulder but the assistant smacked her bottom with her hand and pointed Danielle forward. Danielle wondered if the Duke had seen her and was he smiling at her for what he had seen. The heat grew within Danielle and every time the assistant touched her or moved her to mark her body for measurements her pulse quickened. Danielle closed her eyes and pretended that the assistant was the Duke. That it was his hands marking her skin. His hands exploring her body. Danielle opened her eyes and felt the heat ebbing away and her breath a bit ragged but the blood that flooded her face was washing away. Danielle looked down to see a look of shock on the young assistant's face which turned to a knowing smile. Minutes later, the assistant drew a thick robe over Danielle's shoulders and waited for Danielle to be covered before folding the barrier up and sliding it to the side of a nearby table.

The Duke let Danielle know that it would take the majority of the night for the dresses to be made as well as an assortment of small clothes. Apparently the shopkeeper and his staff had volunteered to work all night to ensure that the goods were ready to go when the caravan left the following day. In the meantime, another seamstress was busy altering the lovely silk dress with the pink and purple embroidery that sat in the window for Danielle to wear this evening. New small clothes were given to her that were a bit too large but were the first new set of small clothes she had owned since she was eleven. Danielle took the clothes into a small dressing room and purposely left the door ajar while she dressed, hoping that the Duke would smile upon her once more. Danielle never turned around and dressed quickly but when she exited the dressing room there he stood expressing how lovely she looked and thanking the team of workers for their effort. He said that he would be back personally by ten o'clock the next morning to pick up the order. The team scurried frantically as the Duke and Danielle made their way outside, and clicking behind them caused Danielle to turn to see that a large sign proclaiming the store closed until further notice flat against the big storefront window. Three women rushed past them in the street and knocked on the door. The assistant let them in and slammed the door shut. The Duke seemed not to notice or just did not care about the excitement as he spent the next several minutes asking

Danielle about different types of food until they found a purveyor of fine meat pies. They picked out three meat pies and two fruit pies to bring back to the Constable's home.

. . .

Danielle stretched her toes toward the fire and yawned as she found her place in the book and began reading again. Page after page flipped between her fingers until she came to the chapter titled "Grey Myst Isle". Danielle paused as somewhere in the back or her mind a faint recognition of the chapter's title nudged forward. Danielle muttered the words "Grey. Myst. Isle," in a way that sounded almost trance like. A tickle of her brain almost like a butterfly was trapped inside her head flitting about just wanting to find a way out. Danielle absent-mindedly scratched at the top of her head and focused upon the pages. As she turned the page, the tickle in her brain eased as she read of the three failed attempts to navigate the Green Sea to find the mythical Island that was thought to have been permanently shrouded in fog. The first attempt was a known failure as one ship out of the seventeen that set out was found beached some seventy miles north of Black-stone. The most curious aspect of that find was that the fleet sailed out of East Watch some twelve hundred miles further north and nearly two years earlier. There was no sign of the crew on the empty vessel. No sign of the eighteen sailors or the additional ten soldiers that sailed with them.

Danielle found herself compelled to keep reading and she felt her weariness slip away as she curled her knees up toward her chest and read on. Danielle read about the second fleet to head out of East Watch some dozen or so years after the first. It was chronicled that this fleet, complete with three of the largest transport shifts ever con-structed, were being led by two royal vessels and each ship brought with them a Scryer. Fifty ships in all sailed under a cloudless sky through the roiling sea. It was assumed that the Scryers would be able to foretell danger and guide them to the Island. According to the book, after only five days of sailing, the Scrying station in East Watch lost contact with the last of the Scryers at sea. The last contact with the fleet occurred when a Scryer sent two reports; the first, an innocuous report that indicated that that the sea was much calmer than expected, the winds were unabated, and that the fleet found no trace of concern. The second report, however, spoke of a furious storm, raging winds tossing the smaller Cutters about like toys, and a smothering haze that enveloped them from all sides. The second report ended with what was described only as a shuddering wail before the crystals in the East Watch Scryers station went dark. According to the author, the second report from the fleet happened only four and a half minutes after the first.

Enthralled by the text, Danielle felt her pulse racing and placed the book on the rug. She stood and scanned the room until she found the wine bottle sitting on the bed side table. Danielle ran to the table and grabbed the bottle. She thought of filling the glass that sat idly on the same table. She took the wine from but instead took a healthy swig of the drink straight from the bottle. After a long sip, Danielle wiped away the wine from the corner of her mouth and carried it back to her spot on the rug. Danielle needed to know what happened next.

After reading ten pages discussing the virtues of exploring the edges of the world, the author detailed the third and final time Tantra tried to get to Grey Myst. The journey took place some four hundred years ago but the author wrote that this was purely a militarily devised plan. Apparently, it was thought that some ghost like force had attacked the country and after outcries for justice by families from Tantra and Wintersbane, the new King Sorling had allowed for a joint attack to be mounted from both Blackstone and East Watch. More than one hundred ships sailed from Blackstone alone and another sixty from East Watch. All warships equipped with the most modern of weaponry and manned by the last remnants of loyal soldiers who were not a part of the War for Dorias the year before. The soldiers on the

Tantra vessels came mainly from the group of defenders known as the Shield of the Homeland who were stationed ninety miles north of the safe haven Splendor. From Wintersbane, the forces were a combination of the black metal wielding warriors that lived near Blackstone Gorge just north of the Hearts of Fire. The ore mined in the gorge was transported by the ton to the aptly named city Forge. Forge was one of the cities known as the Twins with the nation's capital Castleton sitting on the other side of Howler Bay across the giant stone and metal bridge built during the time of the First World. In Forge, a permanent sooty haze clouded the lower sky as the crafters and martial artisans who manned the Metal Works spent sunrise to sunset crafting weapons and armor, and ship fittings from the dense dark ore that could only be found near Blackstone. After the fall of the Ottrun family line at the War for Dorias, many families, including some from Tantra, fought for control of Wintersbane. Each family wished to show they were more deserving of the next to ascend the throne and, in a sign of how devoted they were, volunteered more and more soldiers, sailors, and money to the cause.

The ships from Blackstone sailed four days ahead of the East Watch fleet in order to meet up with them just south of where the Isle was purported to be. The lead vessel and the trail vessel from the Tantra fleet carried a Scryer, while the Wintersbane fleet dropped a specially colored buoy every twenty nautical miles in case a rescue fleet was needed to track them. Frustratingly, the book ended on the next page with a simple recount that neither fleet was heard from again. Where, Danielle wondered, was the follow up? Did anyone look for them? What about the buoys? Has anyone made the attempt in the last four hundred years? So many questions raced through Danielle's mind that she did not notice the sunrise and she did not notice that one of the Duke's servants was standing at attention waiting for Danielle to acknowledge her. Danielle startled when she stood up and saw the servant smiling at her. After composing herself Danielle allowed the servant to escort her to the bath where she handed the servant her night clothes and slinked into the deep basin. Soap was added and with a paddle the servant churned the water until it foamed with bubbles. Danielle held some bubbles in her hand and the majority of the foam spilled over thumb bringing her back to that fateful day.

• • •

"Fashionably late," the Constable bellowed as the Duke and Danielle entered the dining hall presenting the variety of pies with a flourish. The assembled group laughed at the gesture with the Dock Master offering a very subdued "heh, heh". With all seated, the Duke regaled everyone with the joyous romp through North Watch that Danielle experienced. The Duke did not fail to notice the discomfort he was causing Averill by doting on his daughter. In fact, the Duke relished the notion that he had the Dock Master twisting in the wind. The Duke purposely used any chance to place his hand on Danielle's or to pat her upon the shoulder with a knowing look. Any opportunity to keep Danielle focused upon him and in turn to tighten Averill's collar a bit. Truly just a game for the Duke with maybe a trace of actual interest in the girl. The Duke took a moment to size up Danielle and thought that she will make a beautiful woman, but at thirteen, she was still a girl regardless of what her nurse said about her being a "woman grown". As the meal wound down and the dessert pies were brought out, the Duke had stood and gave a thoughtful toast. He poured a special drink that he said he had found during a rare trip to the South. The drink was fruitier than the wine they were accustomed to and it fizzed with bubbles. So much so that when a second bottle needed to be opened by the Duke he asked Danielle to hold the bottle while he uncorked it, a stream of fizz burst from the bottle and cascaded over Danielle's thumb. When dessert was over, the Dock Master instructed Danielle to go to bed in order to be ready for the long trip back the next day. The Duke interjected that it would be important for the group to wait until he returned with Danielle's gifts, and that he would take it as a personal insult if Averill left prematurely.

Danielle said her good nights and lingered near the Duke for a moment longer than the Dock Master would have liked and a moment shorter than what she would have liked. The Duke thanked her for being such wonderful company and that he would see her in the morning. Danielle took a long time to undress as she readied for bed as she spent much of her time fantasizing about being swept up into the Duke's arms and bedded like a woman grown. Danielle even peeked outside her door twice hoping to see the Duke, but he was still at the table in the middle of quite a lively discussion about some future trip outside of the realm. Intrigued, Danielle cupped her ear to better hear the men talk and she discerned that the Duke as fascinated with finding something or someone called the Dagenskur. The other men seemed to hush at the name, and the Duke seized the moment to drive his point across that not only could he ensure that he knew where they would be found but what it would take to defeat them. The men were subdued by the tenor of the exchange and the Duke challenged them to disagree if thought they knew better. Danielle started to tune out the majority of the exchange and strained to hear the Duke. As she listened more to the sound of his voice rather than the words spoken, Danielle felt the blood rush and tingling that had nearly overcome her when she was being attended to by the dress maker's assistant behind the changing screen. She rushed to explore those feeling more intimately in the safety of her bed. As she was closing the door to her room she heard the Duke clearly state that if he could not get to Grey Myst Isle to meet the Dagenskur he knew how to bring them to Dorias.

• • •

Danielle was dried by the servant outside of the bath determined to find out what happened to the third fleet, and could not wait until supper was served to ask Randall all about it. Danielle never called the Duke by his first name except when they shared a bed. In bed was where the Duke shared his name the first time two years earlier in celebration of her fifteenth name day in a room at the Constable's home in North Watch. Danielle thought wistfully at the memory of offering herself to the Duke that night while wearing one of the dresses he had made for her during her first visit. A wry smile crossed her face as she thought of the way the Duke had said goodbye to her and her father that first trip.

. . .

As the sun tried to break through the cloud filled sky, the Dock Master finished inspecting the wealth of goods that nearly overflowed from the six carts. Fresh horses, yearlings possibly, but more than a hand taller than the haulers hooked to his own carts snorted a greeting as he passed by. The Dock Master had always thought that they had returned with a better than fair exchange, as per the agreement with the Duke so many years earlier but as he stared at this assortment he knew that he should have gotten so much more. Irritated at the thought that the Duke had misled him he did not have to be asked to wait for the Duke's return. He had no intention of leaving without complaint. The Dock Master was even more expectant of the Duke's return than his daughter Danielle. That, the Dock Master thought with a sneer, was something considering that his daughter all but lay on the dining table to be served as the main course for the man.

As the time passed, the Dock Master grew anxious and paced next to his team of horses. The sun was not overhead yet so he still had plenty of days to use on the way home and could be far enough down the Northern Trail to be away from the majority of bandits that prey on the eastern side of Trader's Bridge. The Dock Master heard Danielle call out from the porch and saw the Duke's carriage reach the guard house. As the carriage rolled to a halt, Danielle flashed past her father and opened the door. From the carriage two women stepped out before the Duke and each held a beautiful dress. Danielle looked at the dresses and asked the women, "May I touch them?" To which the Duke replied "They are your dresses. You may do whatever you want with them." Danielle glowed as she stroked the body of one dress and the sleeve of the other. They were lightly jeweled and embroidered and made from the smoothest, softest fabric Danielle had ever touched. Danielle teared up. The Duke showed genuine concern when he asked "if you are not happy, I will see to it that they start again." "No, no, no they are wonderful. So beautiful. Thank you. This is the nicest gift I've ever gotten." Danielle gushed to the dismay of her father. The Duke righted himself and smiled proudly, then knocked on the carriage door which opened to see two more women step out, each with a dress on their arm. A fifth and final woman held a large bag and she held it open so Danielle could see the numerous small clothes and a sheer robe. At the very bottom of the bag were her own clothes, darned and cleaned.

"I need a word with you, Duke," the Dock Master's words pierced the moment like a dagger popping a balloon. "And I, you, Averill," was the Duke's retort. The two men stepped up on the porch out of ear shot of the group, and the Dock Master spoke firmly but quite respectfully, as the time waiting for the Duke's return soothed his anger. He asked about this year's exchange versus the prior years, to which the Duke exclaimed his concern that the Constable had failed him and that he would make it up to Crescent Bay. The Dock Master was taken aback by the response and bowed his head in thanks. The Duke then called for the Constable to join them on the porch, and when he did the Duke spoke plainly and directly reminding the Constable of his duty to the Duke, and that he had failed to provide the services to Crescent Bay as required. The Constable begged forgiveness and pleaded ignorance as to the mistreatment of the guests on prior visits. The Duke then said, "Going forward, Crescent Bay shall visit four times yearly and each time you will make them your most precious of guests and you will see to it that they leave with the same kind of trade as they have today".

The Duke turned to the Dock Master and asked, "Is that arrangement fair to you?" The Dock Master happily answered. "More than fair." Speaking to the Constable, the Dock Master implored his understanding, "Constable, you have been a fine host and I thank you for your hospitality. Please do not think that I blame you for anything. You have done us a great service this visit and I hope to repay you in kind." The Constable looked to the Duke before answering, "I run this town and how the traders treated you is my responsibility. It will never happen again and you and your companions are welcome under this roof whenever you call upon me."

The Duke smacked his hands together and then dismissed the Constable. When the Constable left the porch the Duke whispered to the Dock Master that upon his next trading visit "there may well be a new Constable, but not to fret as there will not be any confusion as to what you shall leave here with ever again. To that point, when you or your people return I need your promise that Danielle will travel with them. That will allow me to better know her. I would ask that one week prior to starting out you will send a villager to the local Scrying Station to inform me so that I may have the lead time to arrive when Danielle does. I will also tell you that each visit must last three days at a minimum." Chagrined, the Dock Master asked, "What are your intentions with my daughter? Are they honorable?" The Duke stroked his chin in thought and said, "I am always honorable, sir. My word is my bond and my word is that I wish to know if Danielle would be suitable to marry. I will not simply be taken in by her fetching looks and, shall I say, her eagerness. No, I need to see if she could be more than a fish monger's daughter. I need to know if she could handle herself at Court. I also will let you know that she is still very much a child and I do not want a child. I want a woman. If she becomes who I need her to be then you will be moving up in society." The Dock Master nodded curtly in understanding and held his hand out to the Duke who grasped it and hissed. "I will also say that if you do not see our bargain through unto its completion that young impressionable Danielle will be selling herself for crusts of bread." The Duke did not let the Dock Master interject as he continued. "I have heard that you have taken a real liking to the boy and that you have allowed Danielle to be smitten with him. Let me be clear, Averill, that boy must leave on his eighteenth name day. He must receive no blessing and he must be cast out. If you have not already done so, I would invite your most trusted and explain the situation in order to make sure no home makes the mistake of claiming the boy. There will likely be questions anyway with your magnificent return of goods and with your more frequent trips coming up."

Before the Duke let the Dock master leave the porch he made one more request. This request was dangerous and illegal. The Duke said that "once each year for the next four years that someone will have to sail to Blackstone to collect a massive supply of black metal weapons and armor." The Duke assured the Dock Master that the travel will not be impeded by the Cutters, but he could not guarantee that the Ghost Fleet, Wintersbane's presence in the Green Sea, would not be a hazard. Also a concern is the rough sea itself. Many a ship had been sucked to the ocean floor on even the prettiest of days. The Duke casually mentioned that the first shipment would be available to pick up in four months and that it would take at least three ships to carry the load. The Dock Master chewed on those words a moment and, after a deep breath, agreed. Glorious," the Duke exclaimed as he bounded from the steps toward Danielle. "You, my dear," the Duke offered, "will have so much to talk about with your father on your trip home. Until we meet again."

The Dock Master climbed onto the cart and called to the caravan "let's go home" and cracked the horses into motion. As they trotted through the gate the Dock Master dreaded what was to come. Danielle leaned out of the cart and waved furiously until the Duke gave a grandiose wave and bow, and then a very subtly blown kiss.

Danielle's heart jumped into her throat and she whispered "until we meet again" and giggled softly, almost dancing in her seat. Danielle turned to her father expecting him to start talking about whatever the Duke meant but the Dock Master shook his head and said only "it's a long trip home and we will talk. Just not now." Danielle frowned, and showed her true age as she sulked. The Dock Master thought "she's still my little girl" and allowed himself to smile for the first time all trip.

. . .

Dressed, and fed on cheese, bread and wine, Danielle walked the halls of the Crystal Citadel much like a Queen would. Servants were always ready to fulfill her needs at any time of day or night. Today was a quiet day in the Citadel. This was called a Reflection Day, and all of the Scryers in Prophets Call would meditate and channel their powers in a day of rest. The normal madness of hundreds of people seeking aid, especially from the Precept, would resonate loudly through these halls but today only her padded slippers could be heard slapping the tiles. In the great library where one would find dozens of Scryers and visitors on any other day each season if it were not for Reflection Day, only the Master of Books could be found among the enormous shelves. Danielle alerted the Master of her appearance by clearing her throat and the master shuffled to her side. "How may I help you Lady Averill?" The Master asked. Danielle described her interest in any recorded histories of the joint trip to Grey Myst Isle or any others since. "I'm quite sure you'd be more interested in a happier topic Lady Averill," hoped the Master. Not to be denied, Danielle made it clear that she would make herself comfortable but wanted enough to read here and take back to her chambers as well. That acknowledgment struck a chord with the Master of Books as it was known that these books were never to leave the library. He fought the urge to add that disclaimer as he feared the Duke's retaliation and went about his appointed task with a sense of urgency reserved for the Royal family.

There were a handful of books for Danielle to peruse, but one book, a bluish hued tome with slippery pages truly captivated her. Danielle had a hard time feeling the edge of each page and in turn had a hard time turning those pages. Danielle thought that maybe the drier air in her room would make it easier to turn the pages and she told the Master that she would be taking this one, but she wanted him to store the remaining six books in a spot reserved just for her so that no one would have to hunt for them again. The Master smiled wanly and waved goodbye, but Danielle hardly noticed. She was more interested with the book's spine where the title "Mystery of the Dagenskur" by Gerrand Morecap was inked.

16

Raleigh, the handsome mute merchant had been both chagrined and excited by the night's events. How a man of below modest means could find himself being lavished upon by the Queen left him dumbfounded. As taken as he was by Yvette's beauty and how commanding she was in her chambers during their lovemaking, Raleigh felt the slightest twinge of guilt as he dared to think of the Queen's younger sister Catherine. Although he had spent hours pressed against the Queen's giving body and had wordlessly kissed her over and over it was remembering Catherine's brief touch at dinner that inspired his morning performance—when the Queen demanded that her attendants watch the torrid pairing. Since the Queen had a habit of speaking while facing away from him, Raleigh had no idea if he was to stay or go? His first inclination was to find his daughter and leave quietly. Raleigh was relieved when two of the younger, kind faced attendants led him to the same bath chamber as he had used the day prior. While bathing, the attendants faced Raleigh and clearly explained what was expected of him today. Raleigh made a mental note of the simple instructions; pack up the kiosk and secure his wares at the storehouse near the stables. Purchase a set of traveling clothes for his daughter and himself and then return in time for lunch. Raleigh nodded his thanks to the girls as they took his soiled clothes from the day before to be cleaned and left him to dry off beneath the prismatic skylight arching above him. The mute hummed a glorious tune—if only in his mind—and awaited the attendants' return. Raleigh was visibly relieved to see one attendant return with a clean, stylish white shirt and black pants. Raleigh more than expected to see his own tattered clothes piled in a heap as a sign to make himself scarce, and smiled broadly with the knowledge that he was welcomed for at least another day. Raleigh dressed quickly and made his way down a large corridor where a carnival of smells wafted tantalizingly all about him. As he neared the dining hall a slight man wearing an ornate hood stopped him with a crooked smile and sad eyes. Raleigh nodded and smiled at the man who began speaking with his hands in such a practiced manner that Raleigh stood mouth agape for several seconds before returning the polite greeting. Raleigh was so caught up in the exchange that his hands moved in a blur, somewhat perplexing the hooded man. Raleigh controlled his breathing and slowed his hands enough to make his words clear. The discussion lasted for no more than five minutes, but it was long enough that when the two men amicably parted, Raleigh found the dining hall empty. There were plenty of hot and cold foods, wine, fruits, and cheeses and one unused setting. Raleigh noted that four setting were used including the Queen's, and he proudly thought of his own daughter, Torrie, sitting beside the royal family and sharing in the meal. Raleigh Corning had only felt this happy one other time—and that was the day he held his baby girl for the first time.

Raleigh ate well, stuffed a full loaf of bread and a hunk of cheese within large linen napkin and tied the corners to create a makeshift bag. He then rushed to his stall to store his wares as he was instructed. When Raleigh reached his stall he saw the same man standing at attention that was assigned a full day before. Raleigh thanked the man by holding his hand over his heart and bowing. He then offered the food to the guard who did little more than glance sideways at it before snapping the heels of his boots together and marching singly away from the stall. Raleigh began packing his meager collection onto the rickety cart he had propped up against the wall. He folded the last section of the stall and leaned it next to the cart. Assured that he had left nothing of use behind, Raleigh pushed the cart down Protector's Road. At the storehouse, a weathered old man so wrinkled that his forehead sagged over the tops of his eyes greeted Raleigh with nary a sound. The old man spied the collection, no doubt looking for something to skim as a security payment when the hooded man from the palace stepped between them. The old man's cheeks burned flushed with fear as the hooded man spoke softly into his ear. Raleigh clutched the handles of his cart in worry when the hooded man turned effortlessly and made his hands flow with a story of assurance that his goods will be kept secured and that neither prying eyes nor hands will ever near them.

The old man guided Raleigh and the hooded man to a small vault just large enough to hold the cart and the belongings. Once inside, the old man closed the heavy door so soundly that Raleigh could feel the vibration through his chest. The hooded man was very happy and clapped Raleigh on his forearm. The hooded man delivered a new message. He introduced himself as the late King's personal scribe and Scryer, Hassim. Hassim explained that as man who could speak with his hands, a gift that he called "signing" since the day his Scrying abilities awoke on his eighth name day, he felt compelled to assist Raleigh. Raleigh signed his name and his thanks to Hassim for assisting him and that he was unsure why he was given his tasks this morning. Hassim reassured Raleigh that everything happens for a reason and that he hoped that it would be okay for him to accompany Raleigh the rest of the morning. Raleigh gladly accepted the company and then sheepishly asked Hassim if he knew where the outfitter would be? The two men laughed, one quietly, one silently, and Hassim signed that he would take Raleigh where he needed to go.

Walking briskly, Hassim led Raleigh through the merchant district and into the second level of the noble's district. On one banked row of buildings there was a simple marble memorial with a hanging garden as a canopy. Raleigh asked Hassim about it and Hassim reflected a moment before explaining about the tragic fires that decimated a third of the city more than twenty years earlier. Raleigh said a quick prayer to him and asked Hassim to lead on. At the foot of an elevated road where one house was more astonishing than the next, Hassim tugged on Raleigh's sleeve and prompted him to follow to a small side street. At the center of this side street was a nondescript storefront with the name "Odelia" carved in driftwood above the plain brown door. There was no handle upon the door but there was a small cord with a knot wrapped around a sparkly gemstone that hung from the stone archway that crowned the entrance. Raleigh thought to himself that the people living in this part of the city must be very rich to leave that gemstone untouched. Hassim signed to Raleigh that since he was the one tasked to find the outfitter, and that he alone must ring the door chime and then pointed to the cord. Raleigh reached up and pulled gently on the cord and for a brief moment thought he heard music. The door eased back and a soft scent of pine greeted Raleigh as he entered the store. Raleigh turned back to see Hassim waving a friendly goodbye as the door shut on its own. Raleigh searched for a mechanism but found nothing attached to the door. He was so intrigued by the mysterious door that he almost forgot about his task. The front room was dimly lit, but as he walked deeper into the store it became so bright that Raleigh thought he was outside. A fire burned brightly in several glass balls hanging from the ceiling, yet when he extended his hand to them they were cold to the touch. Raleigh thought there was movement behind him and looked over his shoulder. It was merely a shadow his hand made when he reached nearer the glass. Raleigh saw no other room nor did he see any person with him and began to worry that he was in the wrong shop. Raleigh stood to leave the room and became disoriented. He would've sworn that he entered from one direction but he saw no exit. Raleigh lurched to one side as if the world had just slanted away. Raleigh grabbed for the table but found only air. Raleigh's eyes deadened and felt a heavy sleep overcome him. One last attempt to open his eyes failed and his body relaxed. Raleigh could not move, could not see, but for the first time since his injury as a boy, he could hear.

A voice spoke as if from another world. It was clear but somehow very far away. There was a commanding presence behind it, and Raleigh could tell by how earnest the reply was that the distant man was very powerful. The man who was with Raleigh, in this shop, spoke humbly, respectfully yet there was a clear tone of expectancy as if this man had done a great deed. The distant man thanked the other and said you will be rewarded. The closer man nudged Raleigh with his foot and spoke aloud, "He'll be waking shortly. Have you done what you've been told?" Two voices spoke over one another but all Raleigh could make out that noise was that they had done what they were told. The man said "here, you've earned your silver" and the two female voices clashed in saying their thanks and begging pardon, etc. Two sets of very heavy footfalls clambered to either side of Raleigh and he felt powerless as he was hauled like a sack of wheat over another man's shoulder. Raleigh heard the man grunt and he smiled on the inside, which given the circumstance seemed to be an odd time to be happy.

"On your feet," cried the Queen's guardsman who followed the command with a bucket of water. Raleigh sat upright, squinted the room into focus and grabbed his head as it ached terribly. "Queen Yvette will not be pleased to find out where you spent your coin," said the guardsman as he threw Raleigh's small clothes at his feet. Raleigh realized that he was naked but did not know where he was or why he was there. As he fought nausea while trying to remain standing, Raleigh pulled on the last of his clothes and boots and stumbled through the doorway where he was met with caterwauling. He was in a pleasure house. He was naked and in a pleasure house. Many girls waved goodbye and the Madame of the house, the venerable Madame

Elaine, blew him a kiss as she waggled the full gold coin that the Queen had given him. Raleigh fought with the notion that he would've wasted a year's earning in a whore house. Yet, as inexplicable as it was, here he was. The Guardsman put a boot into his ass and told him to "move, The Queen ain't gonna wait all night" and Raleigh wretched on the stone path outside of the pleasure house. Raleigh leaned against the building and started to laugh. He heard himself laugh and that made him laugh some more. The guardsman stood dumbfounded at Raleigh, whom he expected was losing his mind before him. Raleigh Corning, the merchant mute, could not only hear but he actually made a sound. A sound that he heard and he wanted nothing other than racing back to the palace to share his good news with Torrie. Raleigh, relieved at his new luck, straightened up and walked ever so wobbly back to the palace, needing only the slightest bit of directional aid from the guardsman which came from another couple of well-placed boot strikes. The sky was dark but given the alignment of the stars Raleigh knew it was right around dinner time so he knew right where to find Torrie.

. . .

"What do you mean you can't find one stupid little merchant girl?" screamed the Bad Queen Yvette to her staff who stood rigidly, gripped with fear. The Queen had just returned from her walk among the commoners in a foul mood. When she first crossed the threshold of the vestibule the Queen called out for her attendants. She made it quite clear that she wanted to know where the mute was and when the staff indicated that he was not in the palace, cursed the gods and men alike. The Queen's eyes narrowed into pinpricks and she hissed orders and threats in succession. The harried staff searched frantically for the mute and even when they were sure that he was not in the palace the staff continued looking. The attendants were chilled to the bone when the Queen's dinner bell clanged loudly. The staff regrouped and made their way to the dining hall with haste.

Inside the study, Ms. Boson had just completed an important session covering etiquette as it pertained to hosting dignitaries. Torrie was allowed to play the part of various men and ladies of the land and she was encouraged to give her best impressions of nobility. Torrie proved herself quite adaptable and sometimes her portrayal of the nobles left Cat and Mouse laughing so hard that even Ms. Boson chortled at the scene. When the first attendant barged into the study and asked if anyone had seen the mute, Ms. Boson, Cat, and Mouse looked at Torrie with alarm. Ms. Boson excused herself and stepped out into the hallway where she could be seen talking to one attendant. That attendant, a young lady who had bathed Raleigh that very morning, peered over Ms. Boson's shoulder and directly at Torrie.

"What is it?" Asked Cat of Ms. Boson. Ms. Boson chewed on it a moment and then whispered that the Queen was demanding the whereabouts of the mute. Mouse sputtered, "Torrie, do you know where your father is?" All Torrie could do is shake her head. Cat told them to stay calm and that she would find out what was happening. Cat left the study and Torrie began to cry. Mouse hurried to Torrie's side and hugged her tightly. Ms. Boson peeked out into the hall and muttered to herself as the staff called out loudly. Ms. Boson snickered as she came back into the study and Mouse said rather indignantly "how can you laugh? Something is wrong!" Ms. Boson clutched her hands together and said "because my little Queen to be, those fools are yelling at the top of their lungs hoping a man who cannot hear nor speak will answer." Even Torrie smiled at the sentiment but that was short lived as Cat returned. "We must leave. NOW!" Cat cried. "What is it, sister?" begged Mouse. Cat blurted out "its Yvette. She's gone mad. The mute's stall is empty and he is nowhere to be found. She is demanding his head for abandoning her and leaving Torrie here." Torrie sobbed at the thought that her father had left her.

Ms. Boson was certain that there was no chance of getting Torrie out of the palace and tapped her foot nervously. Cat looked out into the hall and saw two guards talking to one attendant who turned and pointed directly at the study. Cat sprinted to the large desk, leaped upon it, and grabbed an ornamental long sword that was on display above the book section dedicated to Stratagem of War and raced back to the double doors and jammed the sword between the handles just as the guards tried to force their way in. "Ms. Boson, we will have to pick up our training later," quipped Cat and she threw open one window at the far side of the study. "Torrie, you have to trust me. We must go now. No time to be afraid," pleaded Cat. Torrie readied herself and looked to Mouse who squealed as the guards crashed against the doors again and again. "I'm coming too," Mouse challenged. Cat climbed deftly to the ledge and took Torrie by the hand. Cat and Mouse had climbed these ledges before, but to Torrie, the ground seemed a mile away. Cat moved as quickly as she could while making sure that Torrie was still with her. As they edged around the far corner away from the guard house Cat saw the spiral staircase that led from Yvette's bed chambers in the main palace to the old Scryer's station that sat unused in the neighboring spire. The spire was nearly five times taller than the palace proper and served no real purpose now. Cat knew that if they made their way to Yvette's bed chamber that they could use the escape tunnel that was hidden by a trap door beneath her bed. Each of the sisters had a similar escape route in case of emergency.

Inside the palace, Yvette seethed. Pacing briskly, Yvette barked at anyone who dared to approach her. In a most unfortunate circumstance, two young men who wanted to have a dispute resolved were heard complaining to a guard about being turned away by one of the staff. The men demanded to be heard and one even proclaimed that if the King was still alive, their needs would be met. At the time of this contentious exchange, Yvette had stepped outside to clear her mind and heard the criticism of her rule. Waving off the first pair of guards who attempted to shadow her, Yvette walked brusquely up to the nearest of the two men and grabbed him by the throat. Before the man could protest further, Yvette chastised him. "I, Sir, am a devoted ruler. I am a Queen for the people. I am NOT fodder for your misguided slander. I would ask you what troubles you but frankly, I do not care." The Queen tightened her grip and the man reached to her wrist in an attempt free himself. The Queen gasped. "How dare you? You dare to place your hand on me?" Yvette turned to the nearest guard who was standing just behind her and uttered her decree. "Take his hands and his tongue," then the Queen loosened her grip and allowed the man to collapse to the ground where two guardsmen roughly dragged him away. "You, fat man? what say you?" The second man begged forgiveness and expressed his certainty that his petty dispute was no longer a matter requiring a royal hearing. The Queen snipped at the heavy set man, "So, you are so soft that when faced with a real person of power, you tremble and cower? You are no man at all. I find you guilty of instigating a violent assault upon your Queen." The Queen pointed at the fat man and told the courtyard filled with growing numbers of guardsmen that he was sentenced to the miller. The guards looked at each other uneasily as they processed their Queen's edict. The fat man straightened out his shirt collar and made a flippant remark about how his accuser was losing his hands and a tongue and he was going to bake bread. The fat man even started laughing as the guards shackled him and led him away.

Yvette stormed back into the palace and came face to face with Lord Byrr, her father's former advisor who bowed and said "My Queen" the words oozing out in such practiced manner. "I've no time for you, Lord Byrr, or your political ramblings this morning," the Queen impatiently replied as she tried to step around the man. "With all due respect, my Queen," Byrr began, "I believe I am the very man you need." The Queen huffed, "Lord Byrr, I will tell you when you are needed. Today is not that day. If you'd like to keep your head where it is, I suggest you use it more wisely" and walked away. Lord Byrr smiled a wicked little smile as he left the palace.

· · ·

"Hey, fat man, are you full of wine or lard?" teased one of the guards escorting the man about to face his punishment for his part in the fracas in the palace courtyard. The fat man did not respond as they stood just feet away from the miller's gate. Two oxen were hooked to a large grinding wheel just to the side of the grain storage barn and they were walking slowly as a woman dumped a bushel of wheat into the stone well that surrounded the grinding wheel. As one of the guards opened the gate, an older woman wiping soot from her hands greeted them warily. The guards told the old woman that this fat man was sentenced to the miller. The old woman offered a crooked smile that showed no teeth and told the guards to bring the man into the house. Inside, the woman offered a fresh loaf of bread to each guard and told the fat man to sit on a hardwood bench. While the guards wolfed down the bread the old woman squeezed the fat man's arms and legs. She spread his eyelids open and then pulled his upper lip up to check his teeth. "Well, he seems pretty healthy aside from all this," the miller joked while poking the fat man in the gut. The guards asked the miller if she needed any help and she assured them that she knew what to do because she was an apprentice the last time a man was sentenced to this place.

· · ·

Ms. Boson was questioned harshly by the guards after they forced their way into the study and was confined to her chambers until the Queen could decide what to do with her. As it was, the Queen was beside herself with a combination of grief and anger. Grief for the traitorous actions of her sisters who helped the mute's brat escape and anger toward the mute for leaving her bed and her palace without so much as a word. Queen Yvette paced in her chambers with two attendants standing silently by the door quietly hoping to be needed anywhere else than here. Every footfall in the exterior hall was met with a sharp glare by the Queen, the expectant hush deafening as the anticipation grew. Eventually, one brave soul knocked upon the chamber door. The attendants opened the door and Lord Byrr entered. "I thought that you left my palace, Lord Byrr?" Yvette asked in an accusatory manner. "My Queen," started Lord Byrr, "I beg your forgiveness and wish to let you know that as I was leaving the grounds I did overhear one of your guards talking about your sisters climbing down the outer walls and then losing site of them." Lord Byrr continued, "I would caution that there are but a few places the girls could go; the stables, the Noble District or"...Lord Byrr's words trailed off as the girls in question stepped around the final turn of the staircase outside the Queen's chamber. "Go on, Lord Byrr. I've no time for delay," barked the Queen. "Yes, yes, my apologies. Yes, well, the third place would be the servant's quarters." The Queen's look of indignation spoke more loudly than her words. She began "are you telling me that they are in the palace still? How could they have climbed down the palace wall and found themselves three floors above the ground?" "Well," she continued, "are they in the palace or out of the palace?" Lord Byrr puffed his chest and lied "they are far from here is my guess and I would dare say that they were obviously helped by one or more of your guards given how they vanished so easily with two hundred servants and soldiers solely focused on ferreting them out."

The Queen, desperate for a resolution and growing more paranoid by the actions of her sisters, reflected on Lord Byrr's words and warily agreed with his assessment. The Queen tasked her attendants with the job of recalling all staff including the Royal Guard to the palace for reassignment. The Queen then gave Lord Byrr permission to handpick trusted men to investigate any leads as to the girl's whereabouts. Lord Byrr gave one look over the Queen's shoulder but the girls were gone and he hoped they stayed that way, at least until he found them. Then, he would have to figure out what would serve his needs the most.

Cat, Mouse, and Torrie climbed slowly, often crawling with their heads bent low as they traversed the staircase and waited for the inevitable clamber of boots ascending behind them as Lord Byrr most assuredly gave their presence away. Torrie was exhausted and begged Cat to stop for a minute. Cat relented, and as Mouse rested on Torrie's shoulder Cat dared to peek over the side of the staircase. She was startled to see just how far up they had travelled and how much further there still was to reach the old tower. Below, she could hear a crier ringing a bell and issuing a recall to the guard. Cat was emboldened as she knew that they would have a chance to reach the tower without being found. What they could do when they got there was a guess, but she would worry about that when they finally got there. The sun was setting.

Lord Byrr picked twelve men he knew were loyal to the old King and more importantly, to himself, and marched purposely from the palace grounds. The Queen watched the men go and turned to one of the two prison interrogators that arrived to help her find the men or women who aided in her sisters escape commanding, "You, men, have one duty and that is to determine who violated my trust, defied their Queen, and abandoned their country. Those who prove loyal will be rewarded. Those who are dirty will be dead before dawn."

• • •

Raleigh shook off more cobwebs and regained focus as he was ushered onto the palace grounds. Retinues of no less than eight guards, most snickering, framed the mute like a human cage. Just a few paces from the palace steps, the men halted. The lead guard made his way into the palace while two other guards drew their blades and directed Raleigh to stand still. As Raleigh's head cleared he recognized that he was being treated like a prisoner, not a guest, and worry fell upon him like a bear on a wounded deer. Raleigh felt relief when Yvette first appeared on the palace steps and locked eyes with him. That relief was short lived as the Queen snapped. "Bring the mute forward." Raleigh heard the Queen clearly and realized that through his stupor he did indeed have his hearing back. Raleigh stumbled slightly as one guard shoved him in the back and he fell to one knee. A sneer across her face, the Queen leaned toward Raleigh and stared at him with her head turned at an angle. She sniffed near him and let out an audible "ugh" and then turned to the nearest guard. "Where did you find him?" The guard cleared his throat and eagerly explained how he found Raleigh passed out in a whore's bed with all of his gold spent. The Queen stood back and straightened her gown. She turned to two of her attendants who waited nearer the palace doors and nodded curtly. The women stepped gingerly down the steps making sure to avoid coming too close to their Queen and each grabbed one of Raleigh's arms. Raleigh heard the women trembling as they each urged Raleigh up the steps. He heard them chattering quietly about how afraid they were for him and what would happen to his daughter if she were ever found.

"What are you saying?" The words were more coughed up than spoken and the attendants spun about dramatically. "You can talk?" asked one woman. The second held her hand against her mouth and squinted at Raleigh before accusing him "you've been playing us all for fools haven't you?" To which Raleigh could only gasp "no, something happened at the shop," before he collapsed to the cold marble floor.

"There you are," cooed the Queen as Raleigh came to. Raleigh's head drummed and thumped and he strained to clear his mind. A dull murmur trickled all around him like a brook through the woods and his mouth tasted like metal. Raleigh tried to speak to Yvette but he could not form any words. Yvette patted Raleigh's right cheek and a burst of pain spiked from his jaw through his brain. A clang of pans startled Raleigh and he lurched to find the source of the noise. Raleigh was bound to a counter and Yvette walked all along the counter running her hands over his body much like she did in her bed. Raleigh fought the urge yet found himself aroused by her touch once more. Yvette either did not notice or did not care about his response as she came to rest by his left shoulder. Yvette stared blankly, eyes he found beautiful the day before seemed beastly now. Raleigh again tried to speak and Yvette laughed at his woeful attempt. "You," challenged Yvette, "mocked my pure intentions with deceit and trickery. You pretended to be a mute and to be deaf in order to prey upon my nobility. You are a con artist and a common thug who would leave my bed, my embrace, for that of the wretches who fill that pleasure house?" Yvette, the Bad Queen, looked menacingly close to Raleigh's face while she spat out "you abandoned your wicked little child while you buried yourself in bad wine and used women. You thought I was so compelled by your beauty and prowess in bed that what? I would not take offense? Is that what you thought? Is it?" The Bad Queen finally acknowledged Raleigh's arousal and climbed upon him. She eased him inside of her and sat motionless. "You gave up this? Me? This moment." The Bad Queen oozed the words while gently rocking her body. Raleigh, tears having formed in his eyes listened to Yvette wishing he could explain the treachery that befell him. The Queen abruptly slid from the table and grabbed Raleigh under his jaw causing such agony that Raleigh nearly passed out. Bad Queen Yvette wormed closer to Raleigh's ear and whispered "what's that? I can't hear you. Has a cat got your tongue?" Raleigh's eyes scanned Yvette with a sorrowful gaze and he desperately wished to prove his innocence. Bad Queen Yvette looked longingly at Raleigh's eyes and smiled while she sadistically purred "of course a cat doesn't have your tongue... a Queen does," and with a wet thud dropped Raleigh's tongue onto his chest. Bad Queen Yvette then commanded her staff to prepare Raleigh for dinner.

The assembled guests stood in honor of Queen Yvette as she entered the dining hall and she told the crowd that dinner was going to be late but that it would be worth the wait for she had personally picked out the meat to be served, but it had not yet been cleaved or put to the fire. In the meantime she urged everyone to take their fill of wine, cheese, and the fresh bread just brought up from the miller no less than an hour ago. One of tonight's guests, her father's personal Scryer, Hassim, begged the Queen's forgiveness and asked for a moment of her time. The Queen told Hassim that she would make time for him after greeting all of her guests and glided effortlessly away to mingle with a group of nobles. Hassim said a silent prayer for Raleigh and one for his master, Duke Morecap. The pieces are all in play. All that remains is to find out who wins the game and after he speaks with the Queen, all players will have had their turn.

17

There is no telling when the massive mountain range was first called "The Orphans" or who in fact gave it the name. What was known for thousands of years is that it was a forbidding, natural ward, protecting the good people of Tantra from the devils and other creatures of the night that lived in the Roguelands. Stories were passed down through the generations that detailed how man who ever dared to traverse the peaks ever returned. How any unfortunate settlements that would pop up beyond the Northern Trail would be found empty, no sign of life, lost to history? In more recent centuries, as the land became governed by learned and adventurous families, expeditions were sent to explore The Orphans for a safe passage while special ships were built that could power through the eerily quiet Gold Sea, or slice through the mess and chop of the Green Sea. Eventually, contact was made with the people of the Roguelands and to the surprise of all was that aside from hard to decipher written language and an amalgam of spoken language that incorporated the sophisticated language of Tantra nobility with the more colorful style from deepest Wintersbane. Added to it was a distinct accent that made common words seem all that more foreign. Soon, trade was developed and under the rule of King Corning an agreement allowed for large castle to be built that would be used as a safe place for trade and safe passage for visitors to and from the far north.

The castle was given the name "Fortress by the Sea" as the builders of the day were much more pragmatic, and instead of flowery names preferred to simply refer to a place in a direct fashion. Therefore, after eleven years of building, when the last of the stones were in place and the castle ready to be lived in, master builder Eaoman Corning, a distant cousin of the King himself, stood high above the main courtyard upon the highest wall and gazed at the sea as it lapped hungrily at the beach just down the hill and charged the idle stone mason awaiting orders to carve "Fortress by the Sea" into the marble placards that adorned the front gate and the wall above the King's chair in the reception hall.

The ships that arrived in the two months that followed the construction were stocked with more food, wine, clothing and weapons than one fortress could need. Or, so thought Eaoman. The excitement reached a fever pitch when the first large group of natives arrived to meet with the King, and they brought with them all sorts of wonders. Bear pelts so large that five grown men could be swaddled within a single hide. Food and fruit and fish the size and style no one had ever seen before. Women of such exotic beauty that the one hundred and eighty five soldiers and builders that remained at the fortress were immediately smitten and hung on every word the women uttered. Even though the men had no idea what the women were saying to them, they just smiled and offered wine and more wine until they all were just babbling and nodding hoping that body language spoke in clearer terms than their voices. The one native who did not share in the revelry was standing in the main hall staring at the sheer enormity of the structure. The man was deep in thought, and did not hear Eaoman until he set a tankard of warm ale by his hand. The man stared at the drink and then at Eaoman where he noticed the rough, calloused hands and damaged knuckles. Thick forearms and neck and a wide back spoke to how hard Eaoman must've worked over the years. The native appreciated how rugged Eaoman was and decided that maybe the people of the south were not all that different from his own.

Eaoman nearly drowned himself as the native greeted him in his own tongue while he slugged down the ale. Eaoman wiped ale from his lips and chin and pointed at the man while exclaiming "you can talk like us?" to which the native simply replied "yes". Eaoman smooched his lips together and then, sitting on the edge of the table whispered "can you all talk like us?" The native assured Eaoman that he was one of a few elders who knew how to speak and write in all three tongues and that he was concerned that this great castle would be used for war on his own people. Eaoman understood the concern and tried his best to reassure the native that although this was indeed a great castle, that this place could not support more than sixty men at any time based on the scarcity of crops and the length of time, five weeks of heavy paddling, just to get a single ship to this spot that would provide fresh food or troops. The pride of being a master builder was evident in how Eaoman beamed while talking about his work. Eaoman acknowledged that had the area been more fertile then it would be inevitable that more people would come north and encroach upon his land. The native thanked Eaoman for his honesty and then grabbed the ale. He sniffed it and mentioned something about The Range before talking a healthy swallow. It did not take long for the native to finish the ale and when he did he told Eaoman that his name was White Wolf and they went back out to join the party.

The party lasted for three days and nights and then just like that it was over. White Wolf and his people left for what he called the Hidden Crown which he said was an eight week march to the East. He did say that if Eaoman needed him for anything that he should send a single rider to Black Lake Basin which, on mount, would take fourteen days. Once at the Basin, the rider should offer these words to the first person he meets: "Air, Fire, Water, Earth, I accept your blessing".

White Wolf insisted Eaoman repeat the words over and over until he was sure that they were memorized. White Wolf wished Eaoman well and hugged the master builder like a brother.

Eaoman had been reflecting on White Wolf's visit when a soldier entered the hall to inform the master builder that the expected supply ship was now two weeks past due. Eaoman asked the soldier if he could spare a rider or two to trace the coastline for a day or two in case they could spot the ship. The soldier said he would send as many as it would take and that he would see to it immediately. The soldier left and Eaoman decided to take a look in the stores to see how much food was left, and he calculated that they could easily make it through until the next shipment-possibly the next two—but just in case he would have to implement some rationing. He knew that although he had royal blood in his veins, he was too far removed from the line of succession to truly hold sway over a hungry army. Eaoman waited until the night's meal to broach the subject with the soldiers them-selves. Eaoman prefaced his concerns with the acknowledgment that he could not force anyone to follow through on a rationing but hoped that the men would understand that it may be a necessity. Most of the men were surprisingly amenable to his idea. A few were more dis-mayed than the rest and they balked slightly, but ultimately realized that they were in the minority and gave up their protests. Eaoman was even more surprised when one senior soldier pounded his chest in salute to the master builder and asked how would he like the ra-tioning to be conducted. Eaoman was suddenly aware that he was being looked upon as the leader. Some of these men had been back and forth to the Fortress several times during the eleven years it took Eaoman to build it. A few had been with him the whole time. He had never asserted himself above the soldiers. In fact he had always treated them with respect and always asked of them to assist only when his own team of builders was insufficient to complete a rigorous task or two. He had been demanding and firm of his own team but had never been cruel and he always worked side by side with the men whenever he could. He was always happiest when he was muddy and sweaty and felt like he had actually accomplished something, not just directed others to do the work for him. Now, masons, and crafters and soldiers alike waited to hear what Eaoman had to say. Eaoman sipped his ale and told them how much was left and what he thought would happen if every man went to a half ration of food and water until the next shipment arrived. He also told them that they could survive the winter on quarter rations if need be. The problem was that even if they agreed to quarter rations, they would be miserable and that would lead to infighting. Ultimately, he feared, there would be civil war and that only a few would survive.

The men all agreed to half rations, beginning in the morning. Tonight they would savor the bountiful feast and let the harsh realities slap them tomorrow. There was guarded optimism as one veteran soldier mentioned that they were hearty and loyal men of Tantra and that they would see their homes again.

"How long has it been?" Eaoman asked the senior soldier huddled around the blazing fireplace in the main hall. An early winter storm had blown so much saltwater up the hill that ice covered the outer walls and the majority of the open main courtyard. "Been six, no seven weeks passed due," he shivered in response. Not even the massive bear pelts gifted to them by White Wolf kept the chill from their bones. Even Eaoman's thoughts chattered with the cold as he had a hard time putting his words together. Eaoman looked around the main hall and counted out loud one hundred twenty nine. Two months ago when they agreed to face the possibility of another missed supply shipment they had gone on half rations. Then onto quarter rations when the next ship failed to arrive. Discord and contempt made easy friends and the men, virtually captives thanks to the ice, began to fight. The first night the storm ebbed, Eaoman and a dozen men searched the castle and found some twenty men frozen to death in their own beds. The most sobering of the finds was three of his own builders; men he worked with for eleven years huddled up together, a final embrace against the cold. That was only five weeks ago. One hundred and sixty four men left not including the two men who rode the coastline searching for the ship who never returned.

The men tried to chip away the ice with hammers and pick axes and then with pikes and swords and maces. Their effort was fruitless and every day more men died. Of the thirteen horses that they started with, only five remained. They were not healthy as they were on quarter rations as well. Eaoman stood, his bones creaking with the cold, and he surveyed the men. It was then that he remembered what White Wolf told him. A single rider, the Basin and the words. Those damn words. They swirled in Eaoman's brain but he could not grasp them. Not all of them. Eaoman called out to the men in the hall and when he had their attention he told them that they must get the ice off of the main gate and that he would need one brave rider to head to a place called the Basin more than two weeks ride from here. The men grumbled until Eaoman proclaimed, "I will see to it that any of you who assist me in this will be rewarded by the King himself. I will also open the stores and give a full ration to the men who get that gate open. The volunteer will receive as much food as the pack can hold. I will personally see to it that the strongest remaining horse is fed tonight and tomorrow with as much grain as it can eat. The other four horses will be slaughtered to provide more meat to get through the coming days." With that, one hundred and eighteen men rose at the thought of a full belly. Those that did not stir were dead. Eaoman turned to the senior soldier who held his hands toward the fire and said, "I'll be the one who goes. Grew up on horses. My uncle is the Governor of The Range. I am Reginald Sorling and I had to choose between war and a nobles' life. Even now, it was an easy choice. Nobles will gut you as if it's some sort of damned game. I'd rather see my death coming. So, if we cut up enough meat from one of the horses we can dry it by the fire and it will last as long as I do. Can take less from the men that way. It's a good thing you just did. We are all dying and they know it. You just gave them a reason to give a damn before it happens. Now, where is the Basin?"

Eaoman recounted White Wolf's story and with a surprising return to clarity, remembered the words Reginald needed. Once Eaoman was certain that Reginald knew his part, he found the horses, picked out the healthiest, and led it to a small alcove off of the hall where a forty pound bag of barley sat. The horse snorted with excitement as Eaoman dumped the bag onto the floor and the horse ate with a fury. Eaoman returned to the remaining horses and picked out one who was more fragile than the others and drove a small sword through it heart. The beast wheezed as it collapsed to its side and kicked twice before it died. Eaoman worked quickly to carve as much meat from the hind quarters as possible and brought those strips of flesh to Reginald so he could dry them for the ride.

Men working in groups of ten took turns battering the ice on the gates until they finally dug through and found wood. As other groups took turns huddling back in the main hall to prevent further frostbite, two masons drove axes into the wood until it splintered. The masons urged those who were watching to quickly grab the splinters and keep them safe and dry. In an hour, the masons had bashed a hole nearly three feet wide and a foot and a half tall through the gate. The masons then shoved linens from the King's chamber covered in animal fat into the hole, and one mason created a groove no more than an inch down on the bottom part of the exposed door. In the groove he squeezed a much animal fat as he could and it congealed just moments after filling it. It gave the door a grisly smile where the fat hardened. A jester laughing at their attempt to live. The second mason had run to the hall with collected shards of wood and with a strip of cloth, bundled the sticks together. He slathered one end of the bundle with fat and he thrust it into the fire where it groaned in response before the room began to smell like breakfast and the bundle caught fire. Once lit, the mason hurried to the courtyard and carefully wedged it into the hole giving it enough room to not be smothered by the big wad of cloth that accompanied it. The masons took turns blowing gently on the wood and the flames grew brighter. The flames strengthened and soon the fat in the hole bubbled and churned. A spark flew upward and the cloth took the flame giving it more life. The door smoked and as the fat dripped down, so too did the fire. Soon, an area more than twice the size of the original hole appeared, giving the men the courage to attack the three feet of ice that cemented itself to the bottom half of the gate. They worked in furious shifts of one to two minutes each. Using every ounce of energy to batter the ice. The gate continued to burn and some of the ice began to soften as the heat built up. Ice broke in larger chunks, and after two hours, the ice was cleared from the bottom of the gate. Two soldiers rushed into the main hall to tell Eaoman and Reginald the news but the cheer reached them first. Eaoman smiled when he walked carefully over the icy courtyard to see the charred husk of the right gate. Several men were collecting pieces of wood that did not burn to bring inside for the main fire and others broke into song. Eaoman felt the wind strike him hard in the face and the painful ice chips that pelted his cheek took much of the joy from him. Eaoman knew that by morning, this wall would be filled with more ice as the spray continued to blow up from the ocean. He turned to Reginald and made it clear that this would be his only chance to go. Reginald grabbed both of Eaoman's shoulders and said, "If our King is half the man you are, then the land is in good hands." Eaoman teared up a bit at the sentiment and responded, "And if your Uncle is half the man you are, then we are all fools not to live in The Range. Good fortune, my friend." The men shook hands and Reginald went to get his horse and Eaoman went to prepare the feast. He owed those men a full ration after all.

Reginald had left the Fortress by the Sea more than two weeks ago. Reginald had guided his horse nearer The Orphans in search of shelter as the winter raged and made the coastline impassable. Yesterday, Reginald's horse died and he salvaged as much meat as the saddle bags could carry and put the bags over his left shoulder. He had lost his flint and had not had a fire in three days so the meat was eaten raw. He had tried not to eat any snow but he was so thirsty that he cupped some snow in his bare hands until it melted and he slurped it down. He could feel his body temperature drop and feared that he may not last the night. As it was, his left foot, which had hurt immeasurably just days before, had gone numb and now a dull pain coursed through his leg along with an unpleasant smell which was saying something since he had not had a bath in nearly three months. To the East, on the far horizon, peaks that dwarfed The Orphans stood like sentinels. Reginald began to worry that fever was overtaking him as he started to feel warm. So warm, in fact, that for the first time since the ice started sweeping over the castle wall, he felt the need to remove his overcoat. He tucked the coat under his right arm and slowly, painfully crept forward. His left foot throbbing now and a shock of lightning began to surge from his ankle to his hip.

No more than two hundred feet ahead sat a row of bushes. The bushes were mostly green but Reginald saw sporadic bursts of color and he could barely contain the excitement. Those were red berries. He could...a shape launched itself through one of the berry bushes and snarled. A wolf, a big wolf, bared its fangs and growled deeply. Reginald laughed at his misfortune. He was mere steps from fresh fruit and a wolf the size of an ox was about to eat him. He couldn't run because of his leg. Reginald felt that if the wolf saw his weakness it would surely finish him off. Maybe, Reginald thought, he should just sit down and hope the wolf goes away. Or, and without thinking it through, Reginald raised his arms and roared till he was hoarse. The wolf had sidestepped from his original position but did not run, so Reginald plopped down on the grass and laughed until he cried. Reginald was about to die, he just knew it and he cursed the Roguelands and he cursed Eaoman for giving him hope and he cursed the damn words he had to memorize. Chuckling in a manic in a 'I'm about to die so who the hell cares' kind of way, Reginald spoke the words but in a mocking, defiant way. The wolf closed on Reginald's position and before he passed out in fear, he could feel the wolf's breath upon his throat.

Reginald opened his eyes and was amused to know that he still had eyes. Amused to know that he wasn't dead. Or was he? He ached at every movement and was able to discern that he was on a cart. He called out weakly and had to cover his eyes when the tarp was lifted and a blazing sun shone upon his face. A friendly face, skin darker than his own but not as dark as those from the southern most points of Wintersbane, smiled at him. The woman spoke to him but he could not make out her words. At least not many of them. She sounded like the group that visited the Fortress by the Sea so many months ago. The woman put her hands to the side of her head and Reginald knew she was encouraging him to go back to sleep. Reginald tried to move to a more comfortable position and could not. He tried moving to his side but the cart jostled too much to stay in one place. He tried his stomach but his face felt bruised against the wood of the cart so he turned back over and sat up brushing the tarp to the side in the process. All around him was grass as lush and fertile as anything he had ever seen in The Range. If anything, it was greener here. He sat amazed and went to scratch an itch on his left leg. When his fingers did not find its mark he moved his gaze from the lush landscape to his leg and felt a sickness well up from his stomach, and he wretched over the side of the cart. There was no more leg below his mid-thigh. He also saw that the two smallest toes were missing from his right foot. He frantically searched the rest of his body and found it to be intact. Reginald remembered the wolf. The wolf must've attacked him and these people had to have found him by chance. He was thankful he was alive but a soldier with no leg is a beggar in Tantra. His life of meaning was over.

Reginald pulled himself to a sitting position and uttered a meek "hello". The woman who had tried to tell him to get some sleep handed an older man sitting next to her the reins to the horses pulling the cart, and stepped gracefully from the seat into the cart and squatted next to Reginald's good leg. The woman pointed to her chest and said "Moon Shadow" and then pointed at Reginald. The woman smiled and repeated herself and the motion to her chest and then when she pointed a second time to Reginald he spoke his name "Reginald Sorling". Satisfied, Moon Shadow squeezed Reginald's thigh in affirmation and in one poetic motion jumped backwards, spun, and landed back in her seat facing the horse and was handed the reins as if that sort of thing happened all the time. Reginald forgot about his leg and Moon Shadow's acrobatic leap as soon as he saw how close he was to the steeply angled mountains that he saw briefly before the wolf attacked him. He gathered he had to have been traveling with this couple for over a week to be so near. Reginald vaguely remembered stories about the circlet of mountains so high that no one has ever seen the peaks for the clouds ever leave. He wondered if this was that place. He wracked his brain until he remembered "Heaven's Crown". If this was indeed that place then just behind those mountains must be Black Lake—the source for the "Old Warrior"—and if you believe the stories, the source of all magic in the world. His own grandmother once told him that all people of the world were born from that lake and that everyone had a little magic in them, but a few had a lot of magic in them and they would rule the world. Reginald never found any magic within himself but he was a determined man, an honorable man, and maybe that counted as his own magic.

"My God, the Fortress by the Sea", his voice crackled with despair. Reginald called to Moon Shadow and pleaded "Do you know White Wolf?" and when she repeated "White Wolf". Reginald nodded, and knowing that she did not understand most of his words held his hand over his heart and pleaded, "White Wolf, White Wolf" over and over again until Moon Shadow grabbed the reins and whipped the horses into a vigorous gallop.

Reginald figured that at least two hours had passed since he asked to see White Wolf and Moon Shadow drove her team hard to get to a spot to feed and water them. Reginald watched Moon Shadow and the older man with her gather kindling and set up camp. Reginald found it difficult to move but he tried to assist them even as they waved him off. The older man carried a large branch and tried to break or bend it, and when he could not he took a small piece of leather from a pocket on the outside of his shirt and fastened a roll of thick fur to the end. The man seemed very pleased with himself and his face creased as he regarded his creation and smiled widely. The man then walked to Reginald and thrust the stick outward, waiting for Reginald to accept it. Reginald looked confused at the offering, and the old man blew air out of his weathered lips in frustration. The old man grunted at Reginald and pointed at him with a bony, twisted finger, and then at the stick. Reginald was about to ask the old man what good was the stick when the old man shoved the fur covered end under Reginald's left armpit. Reginald understood and put his body weight onto the stick and found it holding firm. Reginald smiled as he was able to move around the campsite without having to hop, and for a brief moment felt lucky to be alive.

Moon Shadow and the old man talked to each other in their native tongue with an occasional laugh or gesture made toward Reginald while they sat around the fire eating a wide variety of fruits and sharing a rabbit. The rabbit was fresh and Reginald wondered how they caught one without a trap, as he was certain that no rabbit shared his ride in the back of the cart. They also shared water from a nearby stream that was clean, clear as crystal, and warm. The ground they rested upon was also warm. It felt like this land knew only summer, and Reginald let the warmth seep into his bones. Reginald thought to himself that he was as far north as any man from Tantra had ever been yet he could not think of any day in Tantra that felt this peaceful, this serene. Reginald suffered terribly at the Fortress by the Sea, and for that matter, the majority of his journey that left him without a left leg and with two less toes on his right foot, yet he felt no compulsion to dwell upon the facts. He could not understand how winter had not yet arrived here but he embraced the oddity. He thought it unnatural and wondered if maybe his grandmother was right. Maybe there was magic here. Reginald finished his meal and thanked Moon Shadow.

He turned to the old man pointed to himself and said "Reginald" and pointed at the old man who smiled revealing a maze of old yellow teeth and a stunted tongue. The old man pointed at himself and then spoke in beautiful, lilting Old Tantra "I am Earth. I grant you your blessing". The old man then reached out and placed his hand on Reginald's forehead chanting quietly in his native tongue. Faces, thoughts, and voices pummeled Reginald's mind until it stopped at the image he had when he looked back at the Fortress by the Sea before the snow worsened and the castle disappeared from view.

The old man frowned and shook his head still quietly chanting, and with a look so grave that it gave Reginald goose bumps declared, "Your friends are dead. There will not be another ship for hundreds of years. So many died at the hands of the ghosts that it will be many lifetimes before these lands will matter to your people. Will you hold a place in the high court now that your uncle is to be King of your land?" Reginald was barely conceiving the fact that all was lost for the Fortress by the Sea that it did not register when the part of his uncle claiming the throne was spoken. The old man found it odd that Reginald was so quiet and so he nudged Reginald with his elbow expecting a response, but Reginald was too numb to answer. Reginald sat down on the warm ground and allowed himself to cry as he mourned his men and friends.

The following morning, Reginald bathed in the warm fresh water. The phantom ache from his missing limb gone and his emotions calmed. The old man gave him a sweet smelling plant and instructed him to grind it into his palms creating a smooth liquid puddle. Reginald then moved his hands vigorously over his body and through his hair which had become quite shaggy and knotted. Reginald had waited months for a bath and he savored every second of this. A soft splash to his left alerted him to the presence of Moon Shadow who chose spot mere feet away to bathe as well. Reginald hopped around so that he would not continue to stare at her. He tried to convince himself that he was only being natural, as it had been several months since he'd seen a woman and much longer since he felt one's embrace. Reginald plunged beneath the surface of the water to rinse his hair and could not believe how clear the water was. It was as if everything was brighter and closer. Reginald sheepishly peeked back toward Moon Shadow's position to capture a fuller glimpse of her body but she was not there. He had had a perfectly reasonable excuse to take in her beauty, but Reginald accepted that it was not meant to be. Reginald hopped up on his one leg and splashed through to the surface and yelped like a child caught nabbing a sweet before dinner. Moon Shadow stood inches away, her exposed breasts bobbing gently on top of the water and she asked playfully. "Do all the men of the south fear a naked woman as much as you?" Reginald blushed and stammered, "I'm not afraid of looking. I'm afraid of getting caught looking. Wait! You speak my language too?" Moon Shadow backed out of the stream slowly with her hands held apart and never took her eyes off of Reginald. She stood on the bank, water glistening, hugging the contours of her body as sunlight dappled through breaks in the tree near the campsite. She wanted Reginald to see her. To not be afraid of her or her people. Reginald held his breath as he traced the subtle and not so subtle curves of Moon Shadow's body. He dunked his head one last time and then wrung out his hair. Reginald hopped slowly from the stream to the grass. Dressing slowly near the campsite, Moon Shadow appreciated Reginald's strength and determination. He did not cry over his injuries. He did not beg for assistance. He had a grace even as he hobbled but she recognized that his grace came from within. He was very fit, if maybe a bit too lean but given his struggles with the storm and near starvation, she understood why he appeared weak on the surface. He obviously was a man, as one part of his body responded more fervently than he probably realized. Moon Shadow thought that maybe she should have fun and point out the arisen problem, but instead accepted Reginald's response as natural and she would never mock nature.

Once dressed, Reginald helped clean up the campsite and kicked dirt over the cold ashes of last night's campfire. When he was about to climb into the back of the cart he was surprised to see the old man sitting there instead. Moon Shadow tapped Reginald on his left shoulder and pointed to the seat beside her. The old man smiled and said, "You may call me Twisted Branch," and he continued "you should sit with my great, great, granddaughter". Reginald shot a perplexed look, his eyebrow arched so greatly that Moon Shadow thought it might leap off of his face. "Your what?" asked an incredulous Reginald. Moon Shadow grinned and added, "In our land, things work differently." Reginald exclaimed, "You do speak my language! I was a bit distracted so..." Moon Shadow's grin grew into a full smile and said, "I do, Twisted Branch does and so too does White Wolf. I do not know who else speaks the old tongue but I believe that we will find that there are many surprises in store for us all." Moon Shadow faced her team of horses and with a gentle click of her tongue the beasts trotted back onto the worn path that snaked toward Heaven's Crown.

18

"**S**o," Kahlen grunted, "are you sure this is the Forgotten Pass? Or, did you, maybe forget it?" Ivy, nearly ten feet ahead of Kahlen and using both hands to pull herself through a steep, narrow crevice dug her right toe into the ground and sent a hail of dirt and pebbles in Kahlen's direction. "Hey, okay. The mighty Ivy is not lost." Kahlen chuckled as he wiped dirt from his eyelid.

In the last five days, Kahlen and Ivy proved a formidable pair as they faced challenges from bandits, beasts, and weather that worsened the nearer to The Orphans they traveled. The first night out of North Watch, Kahlen was cooking a large game bird thanks to Ivy and her remarkable hunting prowess. The bird looked like it had been pretty well battered in the process but Ivy simply shrugged when Kahlen pressed her for some details. The bird sizzled in the fire, a fire Kahlen was pleased to remind Ivy that he created out of thin air hoping to get a rise out of her. Ivy did little more than roll her eyes but she did so in a playful way that made Kahlen feel very comfortable. As the night grew later, Kahlen enjoyed the silences as much as when they talked. Sitting on the other side of the fire, Ivy was wriggling her toes in and out of the dirt patch and lost in thought. From his view, Ivy seemed vulnerable, her face softened by the dancing flames, and when she looked up she held his gaze, leaned her head to the left and was about to make some rude comment, that served as the closest thing to flirting she knew when a branch snapped. Ivy was first to her feet and she yelled to Kahlen to move. Kahlen saw the fear in Ivy's eyes and lunged to his right where his staff lay and once it was in his hand he rolled over once and sprung to his feet, letting out a furious scream and pointing the staff in the way men would thrust a spear and a spray of light flooded the darkness. Men screamed in agony as the light tore through them like a blade through a sweet roll. Still more sounds came from the sides and Ivy launched herself just outside of view. Kahlen spread the beams of light in all directions other than where Ivy went and hoped that her path did not take her into the light.

Kahlen concentrated and was able to calm the light so that it did not burn and only illuminated the area around him. The men were armed. Too well armed, he thought, for simple bandits and there were at least a dozen dead. Kahlen called out for Ivy and heard no response. Worried, Kahlen began running in the direction Ivy charged only to find five more dead bandits. Seventeen bandits so close to North Watch. Kahlen wasn't worldly but seventeen bandits seemed more like an organized force than the ruffians who scare and steal their way near the Northern Trail. Slight movement just to his left behind a tree forced Kahlen to focus his light and in the moment his eyes adjusted he could have sworn he saw an animal. A large one, but he shook off the notion as Ivy called from behind the tree. Kahlen ran as fast as he could and feared what he would find. Kahlen called out, "I'm here. I'm here," and slid to a stop at Ivy's feet as she sat, clothes ravaged and shredded but with a weary smile upon her flushed face. Breathing heavily, Ivy asked if Kahlen would help her back to the camp and Kahlen wordlessly cradled Ivy in his arms and lifted her and carried her to the fire. Kahlen shoved his staff into the ground and commanded just enough light to allow him to examine Ivy for wounds. Ivy moved stiffly so Kahlen helped pull the remnants of her shirt over her head. While there was dirt, Kahlen could not see any wounds upon her back. Ivy laid back and Kahlen found no evidence of injury to any part of her. Kahlen fought the urge to stare at Ivy, who felt neither shame nor modesty as she let Kahlen search for an injury she knew did not exist. Ivy was about to insist that Kahlen remove her long pants to keep looking when he opened his travel pack and pulled out one of his new shirts. Ivy was about to protest but Kahlen kissed her upon the forehead and asked "please?" and she let him dress her. Ivy even let Kahlen button the shirt for her. Though she was quite sore, a troubling side effect of using her bear form for such short periods of time, she was quite capable of buttoning her own shirt. She just found herself aroused at how close Kahlen was and she adjusted her position to intentionally brush her breast against his hand. Ivy smiled on the inside while feigning indifference on the outside. Kahlen paused briefly at the contact before finishing the task. He even gave his pack to Ivy to use as a pillow as he urged her to get some sleep. Kahlen swore that he would stand guard and not let anyone get close to camp while she slept. Ivy knew he meant what he said and she closed her eyes. Just before sleep, Ivy thought about how she loved letting the bear out tonight. She also knew that she was starting to enjoy Kahlen's company far more than she planned. For the first time she could remember, she felt a connection with something or someone other than nature. The bear in her needed more time, but that would have to wait. Ivy knew that the longer she stayed in human form the more it would hurt to switch and the longer it would take for her bones to heal. It would still have to wait, were the last thoughts before she fell to sleep.

The morning of the second day found no problems as Ivy and Kahlen decided to take a break next to a small pond. The pond water was sweet thanks to some grasses Ivy named, but Kahlen only cared about how good it tasted and he filled up their water pouches. Kahlen noticed that Ivy walked more freely with no hint of discomfort. Ivy declared that they needed to head further northwest before dark fall, as she imagined that the pond would be visited by bandits or coyotes or both and she laughed. The laugh came out as a snort, and Kahlen wasn't sure why it struck such a funny chord but he too found himself laughing. Pretty soon, tears were welling in both of their eyes they laughed so hard. Kahlen tried to control his breathing and stumbled over his words "laughing? Why? Can't stop?" and that caused them both to convulse uncontrollably. Ivy watched as Kahlen stopped laughing, his eyes rolled up showing only the whites and he crashed face first into the grass by the pond. Ivy erupted in laughter so rich and deep that it sounded like it came from another time, another place. Ivy felt herself go weak in the knees and a primal surge cleared her mind. This was some kind of trap. Ivy was about to just will herself into bear form but she looked down at Kahlen's shirt and decided to disrobe. Ivy balled up her clothes and placed them under Kahlen's head. Ivy brushed hair from over his eye and let her hand linger for a few precious seconds before she stepped back and threw herself forward in an awkward lurch. Ivy landed with a thunderous roar. She was in bear form and she could smell danger.

Kahlen felt like he was watching his body and not actually living inside of it. All around him floated disjointed thoughts and fragmented images. Kahlen could not tell if he was awake, asleep, or dead. He could feel closeness but could not touch anything. He could hear an echo but could make no sound. All around him a haze lifted from the ground. It was thick and warm, and he felt the need to move into the mist's heart. Flickers of movement, hints of sounds, and reflections of someone else's thoughts. A flood of news but no information. Kahlen felt himself lift slightly from the ground. He was no longer tethered to this plane. He expected to see light above him but it was just more mist. Kahlen felt something grab his right wrist and hold him in place. He ached to float away. He tried feebly to pry his wrist free. Kahlen felt himself being pulled down and was soon firmly on the ground. The mist was thicker now and when he looked down at his wrist he could not see through the haze but he knew that something held him. He did not have a sense of foreboding but more of acceptance to the force keeping him grounded. The force tugged on his arm and Kahlen allowed himself to move forward with it. The ground began to shake. Kahlen felt the trembling and quickened his pace. Kahlen urged himself and the unseen force toward the source of the disturbance. Kahlen dropped to both knees when he was certain he had found the source and he searched with his left hand until he found the smooth familiar shape of his light staff. Kahlen stood and tapped the staff to the ground and a soft, safe arc of light chased the mist away, and Kahlen saw Ivy holding his arm, smiling at him and then nudging her chin in the direction of even heavier mist. Kahlen looked at Ivy and smiled. He touched his hand to hers and together they walked toward the mist that remained.

Ivy growled at the two men as they circled her and the prone Kahlen. Ivy wished that Kahlen was awake as she was still not fully recovered from the effects of the spell or drug that afflicted them both. Ivy reasoned that her special gift as a changer allowed her to fight on. The men closed, they were talking to each other and as Ivy shook out the cobwebs from her mind she caught pieces of their conversation. The man circling to her right was short with very thick legs and held a thick net with barbed ends that he hoped to snare Ivy with. The man to her right was tall, and he walked in side step fashion holding a long spear that wobbled as he moved. A third man, just outside of view, was yelling orders. Ivy strained to listen and heard him say "the boy must not be harmed. The bear should be taken alive." Ivy hunched up and took two giant strides and stood directly over Kahlen. Ivy roared in challenge at the man with the net and he looked at the spear man for advice. Neither one encroached further and they waited as the third man came closer. He was a slight man, hooded and had an unusual feel and smell as Ivy bared her teeth. The slight man came up with his palms held up and greeted Ivy "I am not here to harm either of you. I am here to make sure Kahlen stays on his path. At some point you must allow Kahlen to go on his own. His destiny lies in Splendor not in some thatched roof hovel with you. My master worries about you heading to the Forgotten Pass. You were given your orders a long time ago and you must uphold your end of the bargain."

Ivy closed her eyes and changed back into her human form much to the delight of the two men still angling to attack. The hooded man held up his left hand and dismissed the others. The hooded man never wavered, fixated solely on Ivy's eyes. Ivy, certain that the other men were out of ear shot whispered, "I know my job. The Duke made it clear that this one needed to learn how to be a hero before I let him go. He is not there yet and he has a long time yet until he makes his way to Splendor. There is good in him but he is not yet great. Tell the Duke that I still honor my bargain but losing me now would weaken him, and he would never be the man he needs." The hooded man contemplated Ivy's words and reminded her that the only thing keeping her lands free and her people safe is completing this task. He reiterated that the complete might of the land would sail to the Roguelands and wipe out everyone and that the Duke himself would see to it that the last vestiges of pure magic would be snuffed like a candle.

Ivy whispered once more "this boy will be ready. He will need to travel to the Fortress by the Sea. He will need to experience a great winter in order to be the hardened man the Duke needs." The hooded man said, "Kahlen must be in Splendor in one year. If he is not ready then all will be lost. If you defy the Duke, retribution will be swift and severe. I will inform the Duke. Do not; I repeat, do not fail him." With that, the hooded man stepped backwards, bowed his head and walked away. Ivy looked at Kahlen and mouthed the words "I'm sorry" then grabbed her clothes from beneath Kahlen's head, dressed, and sat at Kahlen's side hoping he would wake up soon.

Kahlen and Ivy glided more then walked toward the mist that still clung in this area and slowed only when they heard a girl's laugh. Little footfalls in the mist all around them and a quick glimpse of a dirty white dress clued Kahlen and Ivy that they were not alone. There was a sense of purity to this spot and Ivy held her hand out. Once, then twice, a piece of fabric brushed Ivy's hand until a little girl said "Hello" and stepped right in front of them. Ivy asked "who are you?" To which the little girl just shook her head and hushed Ivy with a finger to her lips. The little girl smiled sweetly and hugged Ivy's arm before taking her hand. Kahlen's staff vibrated and he tapped it on the ground and once more the mist lifted. Not far ahead was another thick cloud and the three looked at one another and instinctively headed in that direction.

In the new cloud, the mist parted as they walked, and they immediately came upon another girl not much older than the one they just met. Kahlen guessed that the girl was ten years old or so, and she sat on the ground holding her knees close to her chest and was crying softly. As Kahlen approached the girl she spun about and scrambled backwards into the mist. The mist did not want the girl to disappear as a path to her opened wherever she ran. The little girl who was holding Ivy's hand waved to the new girl and she rushed forward, hugging the other girl so tightly that neither could breathe. Ivy asked this girl her name and she too made the hush sign with her finger to her lips and then joined her hand in the other girl's free hand. Kahlen tapped the floor and the mist disappeared once more. They scanned all around and at first saw nothing else, but the second little girl pointed ahead and to the right so they all glided in that direction.

They glided for a long time until they came upon a mini storm cloud that hung just above a young woman kneeling in prayer, her hands clasped to her chest. Lightning flashed brilliantly, leaving brief traces of light etched into the cloud and a slow, low rumble of thunder shook the very ground. Rain fell steadily though the woman either did not care or did not notice. Kahlen tapped his staff but nothing happened. The second girl they found pulled the group into the storm and hugged the woman with one hand around her neck. The woman looked at the girl as if she was familiar but could not quite place her. The woman stood, her sheer white gown pressed against her body by the rain in a manner that even Ivy appreciated. She scanned the group before her. The girl who hugged her gave her a wave and blew a kiss to her; the next girl smiled broadly and mouthed a wordless greeting. The tall, exotic beauty stared at her with a hint of disapproval and the man, oh, the man, he stood there like a heroic statue. He was tall, thickly muscled and had the look of a man of measure. The woman from the storm was being waved to by the second girl. Her first inclination was to hold her hand but at the last second she whirled and strode to the man's left making sure the exotic woman knew her intentions and grabbed the man's left arm.

Kahlen looked to Ivy who was scowling at the woman and the urge to glide forward compelled them all. On the horizon swayed a black mass that seemed to stretch to infinity, and as the group slid closer a strange hum turned chant and they found themselves amidst countless rows of wild eyed men. These men chanted in a never before heard tongue and they swayed violently until the very ground split apart, scores of men falling into a vast emptiness. The maw widened and the world groaned its complaint. Pebbles began to scatter over the canyon and eventually they carried all the way to a glowing dot somewhere in the middle of the gap. Kahlen felt the grips loosen from either arm and saw that he stood alone on the precipice. He had the urge to step into the abyss, and as he stretched one foot out he expected to tumble into nothingness. Instead, he foot found a hold on the pebbles and he strode forward. He took step after step but moved nowhere. Kahlen looked back to see his group but they were not there. He turned his attention forward only to find one of the strange men kneeling before him. Although the man did not speak, Kahlen could hear the man inside of his head. The strange man looked up, his eyes black and the voice in Kahlen's head rung out. "A child of earth and fire will protect. A child of air and water will vanquish the demons. The child of the four elements will rule them all." Kahlen watched the man step to the edge of the pebble bridge and as he let his body fall a dire warning rattled through Kahlen's mind; "Beware the child who is not a child. She is death."

"Wake up, damn you," cried Ivy. She had sat beside Kahlen for so long that the first sign of dawn sprinkled pink ink spots along the horizon. Ivy feared that the hooded man had cast a permanent spell, but as she rocked Kahlen's head in her lap and pleaded for the gods to listen to her call, Kahlen choked out the words "She is death". Ivy ran her hands over Kahlen's face and traced Kahlen's lips with her thumb. Kahlen moved his legs a bit and craned his neck to the side creating an audible crunch sound as he stretched. His mind was a bit foggy and he had a sour taste in his mouth. Ivy said "drink this" and poured a handful of water into his mouth. Kahlen asked for more water and Ivy poured some more into her hand and rested her palm next to Kahlen's lips so he could drink again. Kahlen's lips paused briefly in what Ivy thought to be a kiss sending a shiver from her hand to her heart. "Are you with me, boy?" Ivy asked. Kahlen coughed and sputtered then cleared his throat. "What happened?" Ivy scrunched her fingers through Kahlen's hair then lied, "There were bandits. One struck you with his pommel from behind but I was able to fend them off. Don't you remember any of it? Anything at all?" All Kahlen could do was shake his head and say "No." Ivy, relieved, changed the subject, "What did you mean when you said 'she is death'?" Kahlen scratched his temple where a nagging thought was trying to escape but couldn't recall anything. Ivy sensed that there was something dark simmering and knew that it was not part of the Duke's plan.

Days three and four were less taxing and Ivy and Kahlen made excellent time toward the Forgotten Pass, or at least Ivy assured Kahlen that they were making excellent time. Few men south of the Roguelands had even heard of the legend of the Forgotten Pass, let alone believed to know where it was. Kahlen trusted Ivy but still felt doubt about how or why she would be privy to its position. When nightfall came that fourth day a strong wind bellowed from The Orphans carrying a mix of rain and snow. While Ivy hunted, Kahlen prepared a circle of fires much like he did when he faced that bear so long ago. His staff stayed alit so that Ivy could clean the deer carcass she returned with. Kahlen wondered if there was a reason every animal Ivy caught came back with a broken neck. Kahlen wondered if it was something she learned out on her own or if her technique involved a noose. Not that he was complaining, mind you. Kahlen chuckled out "remind me never to complain about a stiff neck around you," and Ivy responded playfully "too bad, boy. My thighs are miracles cure for stiff everything." On the secondary fires, Ivy and Kahlen laid out strips of deer on the rocks in order to dry them out enough to stuff their packs with. Ivy was adamant that they eat their fill of hot food because they may not be so lucky on the pass.

Ivy and Kahlen ate more than they normally did and checked on the strips drying. As some of the meat cooked down, there was more room for the rest of the meat still leaning against a tree outside of the campfire ring. Satisfied that there was nothing left to salvage from the deer, Ivy hauled it off into the darkness several hundred yards away from camp just in case any nosy coyotes or wolves happened by. The ground had cooled tremendously and Kahlen felt the heat being sapped from his body just by sitting there. Ivy did not notice it—as far as Kahlen could tell—or she refused to acknowledge her discomfort. Either way, Kahlen was agitated. He wanted to complain about being cold but how could he if Ivy was so unaffected. Ivy asked "are you all right?" Kahlen stuttered "yes" as his teeth inexplicably began to chatter. Ivy laid a sweet lie when she said, "It is much colder than I expected. We need to stay huddled close by the fire tonight. Here," and with that she lay on her side, her hand outstretched toward Kahlen who took it and lay beside her. Kahlen concentrated for a moment and the light from his staff blinked leaving the only heat to come from the small fires and a warm body. Kahlen drifted to sleep thinking that he could have been worse off.

Day five started ominously. The fires had been snuffed out by a fluffy blanket of snow. The majority of the meat, although cooked, was frozen, and would have to be thawed by Kahlen's magic staff. The pair trudged through the white landscape half stepping, half shuffling.

A small pack of wolves were spotted twice before noon. As far as Ivy could tell, the pack had not split into hunting parties but rather stayed just downwind, the pack's intentions unknown. The repeated sighting of the wolves sparked a renewed, vigorous assault on the remaining miles leading to the Forgotten Pass. The hours dragged on, the cold and the blowing snow wearing on their resolve. Kahlen argued for them to set up camp but Ivy insisted that they forge ahead until they reached the Forgotten Pass. Kahlen relented when he saw that he was not about to change Ivy's mind. He was equally frustrated and intrigued by Ivy's determination. Kahlen also reflected that since Ivy led the way, he had an enjoyable view regardless of their surroundings. Kahlen felt a little warmer inside and didn't complain the rest of the night.

"Well, we're here," a touch of pride and a lot of moxy came with Ivy's words. It was late, Kahlen wanted to find shelter and he was pretty certain that he was at the base of the mountain on which he would die. There was row of dark green leaf trees, each bent with the weight of the snow. Kahlen spread the light from the staff and the snow gleamed like diamonds against the nighttime backdrop. Ivy threw some branches at Kahlen's feet and she told him to weave the branches so that the leaves faced downward so that the spiky little ends wouldn't jab them while they slept. Kahlen asked for more branches but Ivy said that they would have to make do with what she gathered. Ivy snapped some low hanging branches and broke them until they were small enough to stack for a fire. Kahlen focused he beam and the wood smoked heavily, too wet for a conventional fire but the magic staff won the day and the wood finally gave up its fire. Kahlen noted that the mountain offered a buffer to the wind as close as they were encamped and soon the chill escaped from his bones. Ivy hadn't been as talkative since they were set upon that second night, but she wasn't distant either. She was somewhere in between. Kahlen reheated strips of deer and the two ate in silence. Kahlen was relieved when Ivy settled in to sleep and she held her hand out. Kahlen took her hand and settled in beside her. Kahlen felt his breathing fall into rhythm with Ivy's, and he pulled her into his embrace just a little more deeply than any time before. Kahlen could not see the tears streaming down Ivy's face. He could not see how tortured she was. He could not know that she was torn between protecting the people she loved and loving the man she now protected. Only one found sleep to be blissful that night.

"Would you stop with the rocks already?" A flustered Kahlen pleaded. Day six was as laborious as any week long fishing excursion Kahlen had ever experienced. Sharp, craggy notches were truly a challenge for an accomplished tracker or climber, let alone someone who spent their life on the water. It left jagged reminders across Kahlen's hands and arms. Kahlen's feet ached from the uneven terrain jabbing into and through his soft boots. Kahlen dared not complain as Ivy remained steadfast and attacked the ascent with gusto. Ivy implored Kahlen to stay with her as she found a reserve of energy about two thirds up the steep mountain face. Kahlen struggled at times to keep up and when he lagged behind, Ivy would pause just long enough to allow Kahlen to close the gap before assaulting the trail once more. Kahlen paused before securing his grip on a suspect outcropping of stone and glanced upward just as the first sign of sunset brushed Ivy with orange and yellow strokes. Ivy looked angelic in that moment. Kahlen felt his pulse quicken as he saw her lean, athletic frame tense as she prepared continue the climb. She was fearless and fiercely protective. She was not well educated, but she was smart in a worldly way. Ivy was a better person than he could ever be. Kahlen was proud to travel with her and to call her his friend.

Ivy asked Kahlen to light the way just ahead, and she shrieked with joy as the landscape flattened and the remnants of a rope dangled from the trunk of an ancient green leaf tree. "I told you this was the way," Ivy proudly teased. Kahlen excitedly said, "Let's get up there." The two made great time clearing the last hundred feet. Once on flat ground, Ivy sat with a thump and playfully whacked at the dangling rope with her hand. Ivy spent the next twenty minutes explaining to

Kahlen that the climb was not the Forgotten Pass—it was the way to the Forgotten Pass. Utterly confused, Ivy spelled out how her ancestors used to have a thriving trade with the low landers and that there was a very sophisticated series of pulleys and levers, and a special cart that could be lowered and raised that could accommodate as many as two cows or ten people at a time. It has been lost to time but Ivy reckoned that this rope may have been around this tree for three or four hundred years. Where they sat, however, was the real path. Ivy hoped that there would be enough remnants to the old path that they could make it into the Basin unseen.

Kahlen had set the evening's fire, and he handed Ivy one of the last pieces of meat from the pack. "Why do we need to go unseen?" Kahlen asked as he sat by the fire. Ivy finished gnawing on a particularly tough piece of meat and answered, "Well, boy, my people were supposed to be the last to use real magic and well, you and your stick prove that magic exists elsewhere. Some may be okay with that but most would see you as a threat and threats are dealt with harshly." Kahlen sighed then asked in a despondent way, "Then why are we going there?" Ivy hugged Kahlen about his shoulder and told him that in the morning she would share the tale of a holy place built by brave men from Tantra. She would tell him all about the Fortress by the Sea.

19

Heaven's Crown loomed straight ahead, its peaks lost to the clouds yet strangely devoid of snow. Reginald noted how sparsely populated the region was, even though the land was lush and fresh water abundant. Moon Shadow asked Reginald, "What do you think of my home?" Reginald replied "the land is breathtaking. Is it just you and Twisted Branch that lives here?" Twisted Branch laughed so hard that he scooted forward in the cart, while Moon Shadow shook her head incredulously. Reginald was perplexed. He wondered what he said that was so funny, and he peered along both sides of the cart to see if he had missed a settlement along the way. Certain that he had not missed anything, he asked again. Moon Shadow mocked him when she said, "Did the frost take your eyes along with your leg?" She laughed with mischief in her eyes. Reginald took the good natured ribbing well and continued to scan all around. Reginald leaned toward the back of the cart and asked Twisted Branch "what have I missed?" Twisted Branch said, "There is more than one way to look for what is not there." Reginald was not sure if he was supposed to know what that meant and threw his head back asking the Gods for help when he saw it. The village. It was not a sprawling town like in Tantra. It was built directly into the massive mountainside. A labyrinth of interconnected caves with stone ladders and slides carved directly from the rock face and a series of carved steps and ramps that started at ground level and wormed upward at gentle angles for some one hundred feet. At the base of the complex there were large, precisely cut holes that also had ramps and steps that led below the ground. Reginald sat dumbfounded, his mouth agape so Moon Shadow explained what his mind couldn't process. The tradesmen plied their crafts below in the naturally created thermal caverns. Moon Shadow told Reginald about the vast resources including fertile ground that supported many crops, and the rest of the crops and feed animals were on the surface on the other side of the next turn in the trail. The majority of people lived above within the stone. Reginald asked about the open face of the living areas and how the people protected themselves from the elements. Twisted Branch answered Reginald very nonchalantly. "Every day is like this day. We are of earth. We are one with all that surrounds us. The world protects those that serve It." Then Twisted Branch sprung over the side of the cart as it still moved much to Reginald's surprise.

Moon Shadow laughed as she called Twisted Branch a "showoff" and the old man waved goodbye and moved easily down one of the ramps that led underground. Moon Shadow elbowed Reginald in the side and told him "I hope that I'm as spry as him when I get to his age." Reginald faced Moon Shadow and asked accusingly, "How old is he. He is not really your Great grandfather is he?" Moon Shadow never skipped a beat when she corrected Reginald. "He is one hundred and seventy eight years old and he is my Great, Great, Great grandfather." Reginald searched for a hint of humor to Moon Shadow's words and found none. She was serious. Reginald was now concerned. Either he was sitting beside a crazy woman or he was sitting next to a sane woman and this was a truly a place of great magic. Reginald felt uneasy and he hoped that he would be able to speak with White Wolf soon and then he could plan on returning home.

"This is my home," shared a wistful Moon Shadow as she pointed at the large cavern that recessed from the mountain face at the ground level. Reginald looked perplexed and asked Moon Shadow, "Why are you not above with the rest of your people?" After a pregnant pause Ivy explained how the elder family, also the ruling family, is expected to live "where the below meets the above." Moon Shadow clarified her words and detailed how her people believed that there needed to be a bridge between where magic is born and the spirits live. Reginald considered her words for a moment and then, exasperated, blurted out, "You're the ruler?" Moon Shadow smiled warmly and shook her head with her eyes to the ground. "I am but a child," Moon Shadow admitted, "And I will have a long wait before I am in line to rule."

"You will be our guest and my father will speak with you in the morning," Moon Shadow added as she walked into her home. Moon Shadow called back from deep within the cavern and her voice echoed off of the walls in a way that caused the room fill with musical notes. Reginald smiled and looked all about him as the ceiling flashed with light that moved like a ripple upon water. A sudden splash in the darkness brought Reginald's gaze forward and he followed the noise.

The pool Moon Shadow swam in sparkled with light that emanated from below. Reginald stole a look to the ceiling and said "huh" as he now understood how the ceiling rippled. A reflection played tricks with his eyes—that was all. Just past the pool were a series of beds each separated by thin cloths that hung from the ceiling and dragged on the dirt floor. The cave was warm and there was a gentle hum that Reginald found soothing. An easy splash by his foot and Reginald eyed Moon Shadow who floated with her eyes intently focused upon Reginald's. Through the many days of travel, Reginald had spent plenty of time around Moon Shadow in various states of undress, including the bath they shared in that warm stream, but this was the first time he saw Moon Shadow and truly appreciated her beauty. Moon Shadow turned over in the water before soundlessly slipping below the surface. Moon Shadow erupted from the water and grabbed Reginald by his left arm and yanked him into the pool. Reginald spit out water and thrust his hands along the top of the water spraying water into Moon Shadow's face. Moon Shadow leaned back against the edge of the pool and raised herself from the water. Standing outside of the pool, Moon Shadow asked Reginald for his clothes so that they could be cleaned and mended. Reginald bobbed in the water, twice his head went under the water as he struggled to remove his shirt, and he eventually flung his clothes and they landed with a wet slap on the cave floor. Moon Shadow collected the clothes and then paused dramatically before grabbing her own clothes from where they rested on a nearby ledge. Assured that Reginald had had more than an eyeful, Moon Shadow called back "enjoy your bath; I'm sure you're stiff...from the cart ride." Reginald, chagrined, listened to Moon Shadow's laugh until it stopped echoing, and closed his eyes losing himself in the warm water.

An older woman presented Reginald with pants and shirt made from softened leather with a thin layer of fur on the inside. A matching set of boots was then given to him by a pair of giggling girls, and Reginald smiled and said, "Thank you. I think one will be enough though." Dressed, Reginald made his way out of Moon Shadow's cave and scanned his surroundings. Reginald spied the steps that led into the ground and made his way there. Reginald debated whether he should use the ramp or the steps and decided that the lower gradient of the ramp would make his trip easier. Moon Shadow stopped Reginald in his tracks when she said sarcastically, "Going somewhere?" Reginald pivoted upon the crutch Twisted Branch fashioned for him and winked at Moon Shadow, smirked and said "since I am no longer stiff I felt up for a walk." Moon Shadow smiled knowingly and said, "I think we need to do something about that nest of hair on your head." Reginald let Moon Shadow tussle his hair and long strands fell past his eyes down to his chin. Reginald tried to blow his hair from his eyes with no luck, so Moon Shadow took pity and brushed the hair away for him. This time, it was Reginald whose gaze held steadfast and it was Moon Shadow who got caught up in the moment. Reginald turned, imitating Moon Shadow's own movement from the pool and paused before laughing as he lurched forward a couple of steps before turning to laugh.

Moon Shadow stood there and thought to herself that Reginald was strong, but she already knew that from the other day. Today, she thought he was charming. She also thought that he had beautiful eyes. Suddenly, Moon Shadow decided that she was lucky to be born a woman for if she was a man her blossoming desires would be evident, and she would have a stiffness problem of her own.

Reginald felt like he must've met three hundred people during dinner. The food was fresh and plentiful, and although there was no sign of spices, the food was packed with amazing flavors. Reginald watched many native dances and heard a variety of songs. There was a sense of community that Reginald had never experienced before. Even the closeness he shared with his fellow soldiers paled in comparison to what he witnessed this evening. Although each had a healthy sense of self, not one member of this village did anything that made Reginald feel like they thought of themselves as bigger than the whole. That is why when Moon Shadow asked him to join her in the center of a circle made by a dozen or so women that was inside a circle of two dozen men. Reginald balanced on the crutch and faced Moon Shadow. Two men appeared just behind Reginald with a chair made of wood and an oven material, and assisted him as he sat. Moon Shadow called out in her native tongue and two women approached with bowls in their hands. Reginald smiled and they smiled back before they dipped their fingers into the bowls and then brought their finger out and traced their finger across his forehead, cheeks and neck. Reginald could not quite make out the scent, but it was familiar and he smiled at Moon Shadow. For the second time, Moon Shadow called out in her native tongue and this time two men came to Reginald's side and each grabbed a fistful of his hair. Reginald tensed as his first thought was that something foul was about to occur but the two men deftly reworked his hair into a tight braid, similar to that which the men of the village tied their own hair. Over the next several minutes, women and men came forward and each played a part in Reginald's make over.

When the makeover ended everyone returned to their festive activities. Reginald looked for Moon Shadow but she had gone off to mingle or to share a drink with her people and a new face, a wise face, a familiar face, had taken a seat next to him. "White Wolf!" Reginald exclaimed. Reginald wanted to let his concerns for the men of the Fortress by the Sea just spill from his mouth, but White Wolf laid his hand on Reginald's hand and preemptively spoke. "The men of the castle are gone. The winds of ice have claimed them all. You are all that remains. The castle holds great power. Not the power of man but of something deeper. I have felt it. It was just under the surface when I visited so many months ago but the power grows. It grows without anyone to guide it. Without anyone to nurture it." Reginald absorbed the words and his heart was heavy with the confirmation that everyone was dead. His spirit though, there was something that stirred within that propelled Reginald to ask, "How? How do you guide it? What is it? Who will be there? My people will send for us, I'm sure." White Wolf pulled his upper lip into his mouth with his bottom teeth making a squeaky sucking sound and then exhaled heavily. "I was going to wait until the morning to tell you, but there is no need to wait," said White Wolf.

White Wolf edged his chair closer to Reginald's chair and when both were flush against each other, White Wolf placed both of his hands onto Reginald's. White Wolf went on to explain that several hundred years ago there was a prophecy about the coming of a foreign warrior. This warrior would have lighter skin and would be a descendant of the First World and share the blood of the mighty King of Deception. White Wolf continued to tell Reginald how his uncle now sat in the throne of his home land and how the winds told of the great war and how fortunate his uncle was that he failed to reach the battlefield where all was lost. Reginald did not know what was more difficult to accept; that his uncle now was King of Tantra or that he allowed the other noble houses to fall in battle and simply took the throne with no one to stop him. White Wolf also spoke of the most important part of the prophecy. White Wolf told Reginald how the warrior would protect the land's most powerful mystic as she healed the land and cultivated the magic into force of good. The warrior would be responsible for creating the first wave in an ocean of time that would lead to healing the whole world and vanquishing an ancient foe.

Reginald listened intently and respected White Wolf's candor and his belief that what he said was true, but a nagging doubt kept him from accepting it all as fact. White Wolf saw the doubt in Reginald's eyes and invited him to join him for a walk. White Wolf led Reginald back to Moon Shadow's cave. White Wolf went to the edge of the pool pointed to it and said, "Follow the light and decide if my words are true or not." White Wolf did not waver and he continued to point. Reginald relented, disrobed and dove into the pool. Reginald took a very deep breath and dove toward the light. Reginald was not a great swimmer with two legs let alone now that he had just one, but was strong enough to make his way to the bottom of the pool and to see the natural glow that led to a tunnel a few feet to his left. Reginald grabbed the sides of the tunnel and pulled himself as quickly as he could, as fear crept into his mind and his lungs began to burn. He thought briefly that he should turn around but he forged ahead and just as he was about to panic and drown the tunnel turned sharply upward, and Reginald burst to the surface gasping for air. The light was dimmer here, but as his eyes adjusted he saw a ledge a foot and a half above the water. Reginald dunked down under the water and popped up with enough force to get his elbows onto the ledge. Reginald dragged the rest of his body onto the ledge and rested for a moment. This area was a tighter fit and Reginald had to shimmy on his hands and knee for twenty feet or so until he came to a room, an unseen source of light illuminated the interior. The room was not carved from the stone from the mountain. Instead it was a polished marble as far as Reginald could tell. The room held a statue of a woman holding a child to her breast with her left hand and pointed at an odd angle up and to her right. Reginald hopped on one foot until he reached the statue and steadied himself against it. Reginald followed the line of sight from where the statue pointed and when he looked upon the wall his heart nearly stopped. Etched into the wall and covered in gold was a pictogram that depicted the fall of a great castle with waves near it. Soldiers that wore armor just as he had worn were shown huddling around a fire. The next image depicted several men lying down with fewer men around the fire. Reginald's breathing slowed and he swallowed hard as he stared at the spitting image of Eaoman Corning standing and watching a lone rider outside of the castle. After a small break in the images, a new series began showing a man fall prey to a wolf, a man in a cart and a man staring at a village in the mountain. Reginald didn't see it at first but when he blinked and squinted slightly, he realized that the man who stood in the image had one leg. What he thought was a second leg was actually a stick the man was leaning on.

Reginald's leg went wobbly so he gripped the statue tightly until his strength returned. The rest of the wall behind him was not intact and so the pictogram ended. "I have not been here since I was a child." the words escaped more than spoken by Moon Shadow. Dripping wet upon the floor, even her breathing labored either from the swim or from the enormity of truth that adorned the walls. Moon Shadow moved closer to Reginald. Reginald asked Moon Shadow "how long has this been here?" To which she replied "since before my people graced the land." "Did you know when you found me that all of this would happen?" Moon Shadow exhaled deliberately and with a look of genuine concern for Reginald took his left hand into both of hers and let the words slide out. "I saw you as a man in need of help, so I helped. I saw you as a man who worried about others before himself, so I respected. I saw you as a man who did not know what to believe, so I waited. I saw you as a man whose inner strength won out over a grievous wound, so I believed. I saw you as a man who let strangers welcome him in even though our customs are new, so I accepted. I saw you as I see you know, so I love."

Reginald heard her words as if in a haze and with that the world blinked out leaving him with Moon Shadow and an echo of "so I love". Moon Shadow pulled Reginald's face toward hers and kissed him deeply. Reginald breathlessly bit the left corner of his bottom lip and his eyes darted from side to side reassuring himself that this was real. Moon Shadow kissed him more deeply and traced her tongue along the inside of his lips and grazed his teeth. Her tongue probed again until it was met by Reginald's own tongue. Reginald's body had now completely and firmly committed to the moment and Moon Shadow grinned before she said, "I see you as a man, indeed."

The moment was shattered when White Wolf uttered a "tsk, tsk, tsk" and then said "that must wait". Reginald tried to cover his manhood with little luck and Moon Shadow strode defiantly to White Wolf and said, "Father, I have chosen this man as my own. He has chosen me. This moment and this place feel right. Why do you deny this?" White Wolf chuckled and said, "My daughter, you misunderstand. I deny nothing. I welcome this man into our family but it must be through the old ways. Our ways. Reginald must be of our blood, of our people, and of our land. Only then will you be free to love him in such an ardent manner." White Wolf kissed Moon Shadow upon the top of her head and she said "I understand" and turned with a salacious grin toward Reginald before adding "this night, you may need another bath to ease the ache. When night falls tomorrow, the whole world will know of my love for you and the heavens will hear my cries. Rest well, I expect you to be legendary." Moon Shadow crawled out of the room leaving White Wolf and Reginald alone. White Wolf talked first, "My daughter did not believe in the prophecy, Reginald. Through the years she slipped further away from her own destiny. By chance she came upon you and saved you, and in turn saved herself. I see the honesty in you. I believe that your feelings are sincere and go beyond the physical attraction that was quite evident. I will speak with the other elders on this tonight. In the morning you will be prepared first for your naming ceremony and then for the marriage. You will have three days and nights to commune with each other and then...we will talk of the rest of the prophecy. Reginald reached out to shake White Wolf's hand in the custom of his homeland, but White Wolf waved him off and said, "Our culture will become yours and so your first lesson is this." White Wolf placed a palm on each of Reginald's shoulders and smiled while nodding. White Wolf tilted his head to the left and said "that is how we say thank you." White Wolf allowed Reginald to mimic the gesture while holding Reginald about the waist to keep him from teetering over then pointed to the tunnel with a flourish and joked, "I'd go first but Moon Shadow would kill me if you drowned before you were married. I will follow you, just in case."

Sleep found Reginald an easy prey soon after climbing from the pool. The arduous journey, the emotional connection with Moon Shadow, the sadness from knowing that the men from the Fortress by the Sea were lost, and the realization that he was somehow the manifestation of some long foretold prophesy made for strange bedfellows. When Reginald awoke, his body did not ache as he expected. Reginald dressed in the one legged hide pant and then cupped water from the pool, rested his face in his palm and allowed the warm water to caress his face. Reginald ran his hands through his hair and pulled rebel strands of hair back from his forehead. He fingered the braids and decided that the new look suited him. Reginald grabbed his shirt, but decided to lay it over the top of the crutch for added padding instead of wearing it straight away.

He was so far back in the cave that the only light came from the water below so Reginald had little bearing as to the time of day. Reginald secured his crutch under his arm and headed toward the mouth of the cave. As he neared the exit, bright light and unseasonable warmth smacked him like a battle hammer. Briefly stunned, Reginald held his hand against his brow to reduce the glare, peeked out of the cave and let his eyes adjust. Reginald found that his technique had improved and moved far more freely than at any time since his injury. Reginald felt strong and spry. He flexed his arm and watched the muscles coil like the Range Viper, the notorious snake that felled more livestock and men than the Dagenskur. At least that's what his mother told him when he was a child. Reginald felt like he had regained all of his body that had wasted away during the snow siege and his solo quest to find White Wolf. Reginald inhaled deeply and held the air in his lungs for five heartbeats before exhaling. He was less certain, but as he viewed the landscape he could see farther and more clearly than he ever could before.

Reginald attributed his returning form and strength as a sign of finally eating well after so many trying weeks. It was oddly quiet so Reginald searched the mountainside village for any signs of movement but there was none. Reginald called out but there was no one to call back. Uneasy, Reginald made his way down the ramp that led to the workshops and craftsmen. There was no one here. Tools and beautifully crafted robes and rugs and small weapons like throwing knives left unattended. Again, Reginald was met with silence as he called out. Reginald found his solitude unnerving and made his way back to the surface as hastily as he could.

The hair on Reginald's arms stood up as a shadow towered above him, smothering his own shadow against the base of the mountain. Reginald knew he could not run so he deliberately pivoted until he faced a brown bear so massive that he thought it could and most likely would, swallow him whole. The bear rose on its back legs and roared. The bear dropped back onto its front legs the ground shook so forcefully that Reginald was lifted from his foot and forced nearly three feet backwards. The bear snorted and huffed wet, sticky spittle in Reginald's direction. Reginald's nerve wavered a bit as the bear hunched up his fore legs and growled in an ominous tenor. Sweat began to bead upon Reginald's brow and he shifted nervously which caused the bear to aggressively swipe one of his mammoth paws toward his face. Reginald turned, but not deftly enough as two of the bear's claws dug painfully into his left shoulder. Reginald cried out in pain and stumbled helplessly to the grass. Reginald grabbed his crutch and started swinging it wildly as he tried to scoot away from the bear. The bear lumbered nearer to Reginald then recoiled as one of Reginald's swings swatted the bear's snout. The bear roared its disapproval and crashed forward pinning Reginald to the ground. The bear's rancid breath nearly suffocated Reginald and it snapped its jaws shut an inch from Reginald's face. Reginald laughed, first it came as a nervous titter and then soon was a tear inducing and convulsion producing maniacal outburst. Reginald dared the bear to eat him. He repeatedly asked the bear "What're you waiting for?" and even grabbed the bear by its jowls and cursed it and its mother and its mother's mother. The bear cocked its head and backed away, carefully avoiding stepping on Reginald. The bear snorted once and then turned around and walked away. Reginald pulled himself up and cursed himself as his crutch was broken in half. Reginald hopped until he could lean on the mountain for support and then hopped back to Moon Shadow's cave. He found his bed and lay down. Reginald was exhausted from the fight and needed to sleep.

Reginald woke startled as two men jostled him from his slumber. A strong but not unpleasant scent filled the room, or so Reginald thought. All around him sat the entirety of the village. The only two standing were White Wolf and Twisted Branch, and each held a bemused look upon their faces which the disoriented Reginald could not decipher. The men spoke to each other and then spoke to all assembled and the people rose in unison. Reginald finally understood that they were outside, but he did not recognize the view. Reginald stood on his leg and was surprised to find his crutch at his side. He suspected that Twisted Branch must've found him a new piece of wood to work with although it looked exactly like the one he had broken earlier that morning.

White Wolf and Twisted Branch approached and carried with them scented sticks that were burning, which explained what Reginald smelled when he woke up. They spoke in unison and the words flowed like water. They walked in a circle around Reginald and then came to a halt directly in front of him. Twisted Branch spoke first. "Here, before the Gods, and our people you will be named. You will become one of us and you will be of earth, air, fire or water." Reginald remembered that he was to have a naming ceremony before he married..."Where is Moon Shadow?" he asked with his voice cracking. White Wolf reminded Reginald, "First you are named then you will be one with my daughter." Reginald interrupted the men and asked "where did everyone go? I was alone when the bear attacked me. I was going to die." A murmur turned din as the villagers who were to bear witness to Reginald's naming ceremony talked out of turn. White Wolf covered his mouth with his left hand and scratched at his chin. White Wolf questioned Reginald "what bear do you speak of? You have not left the cave since last night." Reginald shook his head in disbelief and asked, "Then what happened to me?" Twisted Branch answered, "Dreams have many meanings but only one who holds magic can touch their dreams. I would think you simply had a reaction to our wine. It is very potent compared to that from the south." The old man chuckled and began to chant again but a defiant Reginald again interrupted the proceedings and this time he yanked his left arm from his shirt and the collective fell silent. White Wolf looked in Reginald's eyes and then at his shoulder. "How did this happen?" White Wolf pleaded more than asked Reginald. Reginald frustrated and agitated responded. "I told you. I woke to an empty village. I went outside and was attacked by a huge brown bear and I fought it off with my crutch but not before it left me with this wound."

White Wolf's emotions ranged from disquieted to pure joy and he embraced Reginald. He stepped back and shared with all that "this man has been joined by the spirits. He has been dream touched. He is already one of us. He is the first to be touched by a bear in generations.

This man will be known to all as Wounded Bear." The crowd yelled its approval, and soon they mobbed Wounded Bear. There was so much commotion that Wounded Bear did not see the bonfire when it was first lit. The mass of well-wishers parted and Moon Shadow's unmistakable silhouette was framed by the flames. Wounded Bear moved toward the fire and all of the villagers walked behind him. When he arrived at Moon Shadow's side he could see the fresh flowers threaded into her hair and she smelled like springtime. White Wolf moved between them and he asked each one simple question. "Why are you here before the spirits and your people?" He looked to Moon Shadow for an answer first.

Moon Shadow pulled a flower from her hair and offered it to Wounded Bear. She clasped her hands over Wounded Bear's own and said sweetly, "I am a child of the land. I am the daughter of a great man. I am sister to all of my people. I am your woman and you are my man and before the spirits I give myself to you and you alone." Wounded Bear adjusted the crutch under his left arm and let the moment sink in. White Wolf laid a gentle hand upon Wounded Bear's right shoulder and smiled while nodding in Moon Shadow's direction. Wounded Bear cleared his throat and said, "I guess that it's my turn." Wounded Bear continued, "I was a child of a distant land. I am the nephew to the King. I was a brother in arms. I wish to be your man and I ask the spirits, your father, and your people to take me into their hearts, now and always." Moon Shadow squeezed Wounded Bear's hands and they looked to White Wolf for approval. White Wolf eased back next to Twisted Branch and they whispered in conspiratorial fashion, and then White Wolf waved both hands far above his head. The villagers all dropped to a single knee and White Wolf proclaimed, "The spirits celebrate this union and I, your elder approve this union." White Wolf stepped briskly toward Moon Shadow and Wounded Bear and then he too dropped to a single knee and said proudly "and I, my sweet daughter, approve of this man. A man who through deeds past and future will help heal our world. A man who deserves your love. I, White Wolf, father of Moon Shadow and now father to Wounded Bear declare this union witnessed and approved." The cheers and hollers were deafening, yet neither Moon Shadow nor Wounded Bear could hear anything beyond their own heartbeats. They embraced and kissed softly. Moon Shadow whispered to Wounded Bear that tonight they would share a bed for the first time and that not even the spirits could save him.

Moon Shadow and Wounded Bear spent three days and nights completing the traditional union ceremony. The pair would take breaks from their lovemaking only for brief naps or a dip in the warm pool which would invigorate them both and boost their libidos so they could sate their growing appetites. When the third night came, Wounded Bear and Moon Shadow were summoned to the grounds outside of her cave. The two ventured out of the cave hand in hand and faced White Wolf and what appeared to be the entire village behind him. Wounded Bear was curious as to why everyone was naked. White Wolf said to Moon Shadow. "It is time little one," and Moon Shadow proceeded to disrobe much to Wounded Bear's dismay, and she smirked devilishly at Wounded Bear before taking her place next to White Wolf. Wounded Bear was confused. He asked Moon Shadow "what's happening?" and she smiled and said, "You were dream touched just as we all were. The spirits are with you always and you will know the joy that we all know." Wounded Bear stared in disbelief as one by one the people changed form, turned into wolves of various colors and ran off in all directions. Twisted Branch and White Wolf turned and howled before racing away. Moon Shadow was the last to turn and she trotted over to Wounded Bear and nuzzled against his left hand before she licked it. Wounded Bear knelt down beside the wolf, his wife, ran both hands over her fur and said, "I don't know how I am supposed to feel. I vowed to be your man. You will have to explain this all to me...eventually." Moon Shadow lapped at Wounded Bear's face and scampered away.

An hour passed before Wounded Bear decided to go back into the cave. He could not believe what he had seen and he shook his head as he took one last look over his shoulder. A deer was grazing on a low bush about two hundred feet from the cave. Wounded Bear could swear he could smell the deer's musk. He watched the deer move quietly from the bush to a particularly lush section of sweet grass where it took its time eating. Wounded Bear's stomach growled and a sharp pain stabbed him in the gut. Wounded Bear doubled over and rolled into the fetal position. The pain coursed from his gut to his arms and leg. Sweat poured from his hairline and stung his eyes. Wounded Bear rolled onto his back and screamed as all of his bones cracked and splintered. His body contorted until it was unrecognizable. Three minutes of agony later, Wounded Bear, formerly Reginald Sorling of the Range and a heroic soldier in Tantra's Royal Army, had become a beast. He snorted and sniffed the air picking up the deer's scent. Wounded Bear had become the great animal that had dream touched him. To his delight, he had a fully usable left leg. He moved freely and instinctively maneuvered so that he could close the distance with the deer. Something in the bushes spooked the deer that retreated right into Wounded Bear's waiting claws and jaws. Wounded Bear pinned the deer and fought the urge to tear into it. The nearby bush rustled and Moon Shadow peered from within watching Wounded Bear. Moon Shadow warily approached and Wounded Bear growled, which the man within the bear found disturbing. The bear leaned forward, protecting its prize from the encroaching wolf. The wolf paced in front of the bear and finally the man took control of the beast and sat, his huge paw still holding the deer firmly in place. The wolf crept toward the deer and nosed it then stepped back, looking at the bear. The bear nosed the deer and laid his head next to the deer. The wolf brazenly clamped its teeth over the deer's neck and shook violently until it snapped, killing the deer. The wolf nosed the giant bear's face and the bear licked the wolf's face. The wolf greedily tore into the deer's flesh, buried its muzzle into the deer's guts, and feasted on the softest bits. The bear's hunger grew and he grunted his approach which caused the wolf to scamper behind the deer. The bear roared and then sunk its teeth into the deer ripping an enormous chunk from its belly.

The wolf and bear, wife and husband, devoured the carcass in just over an hour. When they finished gorging themselves, their blood lust quenched, the wolf and the bear walked side by side into the trees that lined the base of a nearby hill.

The following morning, Wounded Bear woke, dried blood caked on his lips and under his fingernails. He frowned briefly as in his human form he still had but one leg. Moon Shadow stood nearby and stretched. She smiled at her husband and came to him. Wounded Bear tried to stand, but Moon Shadow pushed him onto his back, straddled him and slowly moved her hips until his manhood responded. Moon Shadow held Wounded Bear's arms over his head and told him to let her please him. Her breath quickened and soon Wounded Bear lost himself inside her and they twitched together before she hungrily kissed him and licked the blood from his lips. "Not even Twisted Branch has seen a bear spirit, my love." Moon Shadow's words were spoken in between each of the pleasurable twitches that surged between her legs. "You may be the first, but I am determined to bring as many of you into the world as you can give me." She continued and her words brought a renewed vigor to their coupling and this time Wounded Bear rolled Moon Shadow onto her back and he pleasured her. The newlyweds practiced their lovemaking under the sun and after several hours agreed to return to the village.

Knowing smiles met them upon their return as the rest of the village had returned to their daily tasks and their clothes. Moon Shadow and Wounded Bear called out a friendly hello to all they passed and proudly entered the cave together. They swam in the pool, and Wounded Bear could sense his body's response to the healing waters. He knew that he felt better when he was in the water so he let some water fill his mouth and swallowed it down. His body shuddered and his senses sharpened. He instantly felt reborn and pulled himself from the water in order to dress. Moon Shadow joined him and they embraced, their foreheads touching. They vowed their love for each other and were startled when White Wolf cleared his throat. Wounded Bear grinned at White Wolf who looked pleased with the genuine caring between Wounded Bear and Moon Shadow. White Wolf gestured to the pair to sit and when they did he stood before them.

White Wolf explained how in the morning, Wounded Bear had to lead his daughter to the Fortress by the Sea so that she could heal the land and allow the men who perished there to find their way to their Gods. A caravan with supplies and necessities would travel in the days following. White Wolf explained further how there would be a dozen handpicked villagers who would help them secure the castle and create a living community. Each spring and fall additional caravans would follow. Then, some day in the future, a new pair, one a protector and one a mystic would come to replace them, and then and only then could Moon Shadow and Wounded Bear return to the village. White Wolf told them that the prophecy started with their love and it would be fulfilled the next time a wolf and bear bring a child of pure magic into the world. Wounded Bear turned to Moon Shadow, who held one hand to her belly and asked in a general fashion "next time a wolf and bear bring a child into the world?" This brought a laugh from somewhere deep inside White Wolf, who patted Wounded Bear on top of his head. Moon Shadow pulled Wounded Bear to her and kissed him deeply. She guided one of his hands to her belly and nodded. Moon Shadow's eyes were filled with love and wonder and she said, "We are yours." Wounded Bear hugged his wife and kissed her belly and then proceeded to make love to her until they fell asleep still connected.

20

Kahlen had listened intently to Ivy and her recollection of the events that happened at the Fortress by the Sea. He found the story of the first protector and his wife to be very romantic. He was far more intrigued by the century's worth of tradition that followed. He could not believe how, since that day, there has always been a mystic that protected the land, healed it, and kept it from getting angry just from their mere presence, while a brave soldier protected them sometimes giving up their lives in the process. He was skeptical at best of the whole 'turning into an animal' part of the story, but decided he'd keep that to himself since it added some flair and Ivy seemed to really enjoy talking about the transformation.

Two days after ascending The Orphans and reaching the Forgotten Pass, Ivy and Kahlen finally reached Black Lake Basin. Kahlen stared at the seemingly endless sea of grass that swayed with the breeze. Kahlen's eyes struggled to adjust to the bright sunshine and he shielded them with his hand. Ivy did not have any such problem and she insisted that Kahlen would be better off walking instead of looking like a fool. Kahlen sighed, chuckled, and started to move.

After only an hour, Kahlen asked Ivy to stop. Ivy did so reluctantly and in an impatient manner suggested that he would be better served moving now before it was too late. Ivy had been focused on potential danger to even notice that Kahlen had removed his two shirts and rolled up his pants. Kahlen had known heat but after so many weeks of travel in freezing weather including just a few hours ago, this un-seasonable warmth had him feeling light headed. Kahlen wrapped his undershirt around his head to keep the sweat from his eyes. Kahlen told Ivy "I'm ready" and took a deep breath while squinting at the sky surprised how low the sun sat as he was sure that it should be directly overhead. Kahlen puffed his cheeks and blew the air out as he feared the day was going to get much hotter.

Ivy heard Kahlen tell her that he was ready and was about to chirp at him to hurry up, but when she turned around all of her thoughts became scrambled as he approached. Ivy traced Kahlen's muscled body as it flexed with each step with her eyes. She felt tightness in her chest and for a moment she forgot how to breathe. A flush, not from the warm air, gave rise to a blush as blood surged through her body. A familiar tingling and a twinge of desire brought a smile to her lips. She was both upset at herself for becoming distracted and pleased with herself for just being a woman. She could do a better job of hiding her desires than a man could. Ivy pretended to be irritated with Kahlen and lied when she said "you look like a fool". Kahlen apologized and tried to explain how uncomfortable he was, but Ivy never heard a word. Ivy was too busy watching Kahlen walk by her and all she could hear was her heartbeat as it thumped recklessly in her chest.

Ivy whispered for Kahlen to stop but he was a little too far away to hear her so she jogged silently behind him and tackled him with her hand around his mouth. Kahlen rolled over and was ready to fight but the frightened look in Ivy's eyes gave him pause. Ivy put her lips to Kahlen's ear and spoke so softly "hush, boy. Stay low. Stay quiet." Kahlen was on the verge of being aroused even with the prospect of facing impending danger. Ivy pressed down harder and said "shhh, don't move." and she slithered off of Kahlen and disappeared into the tall grass. Kahlen dared not move and he gripped his light staff tightly just in case. Kahlen waited what seemed like an eternity, and was about to sit up when he heard the first blood curdling scream. Kahlen could not tell if it was an animal or a man that made the sound but somehow he just knew that it was not Ivy. A series of yelps and growls came from all directions and Kahlen heard something moving nearby. Another sound came from something close by and Kahlen knew that whatever it was, it was injured badly. A loud roar came from the grass somewhere behind his head. A grunt and another roar were followed by even more movement in the grass as several unknown animals rushed past Kahlen's position. Kahlen had just begun to breathe again when a large wolf crashed overhead and landed by his feet. The beast spun around and bared its teeth and jumped for Kahlen's throat. Kahlen brought his staff to bear and blocked the wolf. Kahlen scooted backward and sat up while he swung the staff at the wolf. The wolf circled Kahlen, snapped its jaws, and probed his defense. Kahlen took the chance to stand and he yelled at the wolf, hoping it would be scared off. The wolf lunged at him and was rebuffed by a quick swipe of the light staff. Undeterred, the wolf lunged brazenly at Kahlen's legs and landed a glancing blow on his shin causing blood to trickle down to his foot. The wolf feinted toward Kahlen's injured leg who naturally attempted to block the attack, but at the last moment the wolf launched itself at Kahlen's throat. Kahlen only had time to bring his elbow up to protect his face and the wolf's teeth sunk home. Kahlen felt the wolf's teeth pierce his upper arm deeply enough to scrape the bone and cried out. Kahlen aimed his light staff at the wolf and let loose a powerful ray that left the beast in two pieces. Kahlen had to unclamp the wolf's jaws from his arm and was relieved to see that the flesh was in one piece, and remarkably, the bone was not broken.

A labored grunt less than one hundred feet away caught Kahlen's attention. Kahlen scanned the grassy area and was nervous that he could not see Ivy, but was frightened as he watched three huge wolves taking turns attacking a bear. Kahlen started to walk away from the war that raged between animals further up the food chain than he was. Kahlen stopped when the bear made a motion and gave a look that triggered a distant memory. It was the same look that a bear made that night soon after he found out his knife had magic in it. It was the same look because it was the same bear. Stunned, Kahlen urged himself forward and he let out a war cry that startled the wolves and distracted them enough to allow the bear to gut one with its claws. The other two wolves decided to rush Kahlen and this time Kahlen brought his light staff to bear and smite the wolves with a single passing of the firelight before the wolves could find an advantage. Kahlen instinctively knew that this bear was not a threat. He planted his staff into the ground and leaned against it, and just stared at the bear. The large brown bear was exhausted and wanted desperately to run away and hide but could not. Kahlen called out for Ivy, his voice cracking as he feared the worst. Kahlen left the staff standing and jogged to all of the near spots where there was obvious evidence of fighting but the only carcasses were of wolves. Kahlen went back to his staff and yanked it from the ground. Kahlen cried out defiantly "Ivy!" repeatedly and when his voice went hoarse, he whispered her name while he fought off tears. The bear grunted behind him and Kahlen watched as it struggled to its feet. Kahlen looked behind him and hoped to see her beautiful smile or hear her sultry whisper just one more time. The bear grunted even louder and Kahlen spun in its direction and said in an annoyed tone "what the fuck do you want?" The bear bobbed its head as if laughing and it riled Kahlen's emotions further as he yelled at the bear "either eat me or not. I don't care. Just make up your mind you filthy, mangy carpet." The bear lolled to one side and Kahlen now knew for sure that the bear had just mocked him. Kahlen even warned the bear to stop making fun of him or he would be eating a month's worth of bear for dinner and waved his staff all about to show how serious he was.

The bear cocked its head to the side and rolled back onto its feet and moved deliberately toward Kahlen. The bear kept its head down and showed no signs of aggression and looked up forlornly at Kahlen before it leaned gently against his shoulder. Kahlen leaned his head onto the bear's neck and dropped his staff in order to give the great bear a hug. Kahlen did not fear the bear any more. In fact, Kahlen felt as safe now as he did with Ivy by his side. Ivy? The thoughts raced through Kahlen's mind. How Ivy caught food so easily. How strong she was. How tough she was. How she was there for him for all of these weeks. Kahlen smiled as he knew that Ivy was still there for him. Kahlen hugged the bear tighter around its neck and whispered "I love you, Ivy".

Kahlen's words were enough for Ivy to trust that it was safe for her to expose the truth about her gift. In his arms, Ivy changed from bear to woman and she kissed Kahlen on the neck and cheek and proclaimed her love for him. Kahlen said, "It was always you, wasn't it?" Ivy replied with a deep, wet kiss while mumbling "uh-huh". Ivy pushed back from Kahlen and let him see her naked body as it heaved with anticipation. She wet her lips with the curl of her tongue and she bit her bottom lip and pleaded "Please?" Kahlen yanked the shirt from his head and raised the trail pack over his head and dropped it to the ground. Kahlen tossed his staff at his feet and before he could remove his pants, Ivy was upon him and her hands groped his taut frame until she found his manhood. The look of desperation in Ivy's eyes spoke to how badly she desired the man who stood like a god before her. Ivy untied the cloth that kept Kahlen's pants cinched around his hips and helped pull them over his feet. Ivy threw the pants as far away as she could and told Kahlen, "You can have them back when I'm done with you." She kissed him hard and slowly turned her body so that her buttocks pressed against Kahlen's groin and she reached one arm back over her head and around his neck pulling him closer and tilted her head offering her neck to his mouth. Kahlen did not try to hide his arousal and instead let his breathing go ragged with desire. Ivy cemented the moment when she purred, "I want to feel all of you and I want you to taste all of me". Kahlen tugged on Ivy's ear with his teeth and declared, "I want all of you. In every way." Ivy groaned with pleasure as she accepted Kahlen's desire standing there in the middle of the lush green grass.

The night crept up on Ivy and Kahlen, so he used his staff to light the sky and they stayed connected until both had everything they wanted from each other. Neither could lie that they did not get exactly what they wished for and when they fell asleep they were still joined at the hip.

Morning came and Kahlen half expected Ivy to put on the facade of 'last night meaning nothing', but instead she was staring at him with a deep love. She asked Kahlen, "Did you mean what you said? Do you love me?" Kahlen exhaled his hands on his hips wondering where his pants were and he smiled at Ivy and admitted, "I think that I fell in love with you the first night I saw you. I know that I loved you when all I cared about was knowing where you were and that I would rather that bear kill me than leave me here without you by my side." Ivy giggled, a sound Kahlen never thought he would hear and he flopped by her side and said, "I've lost my pants." They laughed. Ivy slid her left knee over his waist and looked longingly into Kahlen's eyes and told him, "We will find your pants. But you don't need your pants right now". Ivy pulled herself onto Kahlen and they made love one more time.

Kahlen and Ivy spent as much time exploring their bodies as they did trekking through the Basin. Ivy explained that soon they would be out of the grasslands and find their way into the magically barren lands that led to the Fortress by the Sea. Kahlen balked and asked, "I thought you told me that every generation sent a protector and a mystic to keep the lands healed?" "I did," Ivy answered flatly. Kahlen probed further, "Then how is the land magically barren?" Ivy said "because in the last generation, the protector died before reaching the castle. The mystic could not hold off the encroaching storm and she died as well. So, the land and its magic returned to its state before the Fortress by the Sea was built."

Kahlen dwelled on the sobering news and then asked "then why are you so determined for us to go there?" Ivy told Kahlen a version of the truth, that before he could face his future he needed to know who he was and believe in himself before he could find his place in the world. Ivy neglected to mention how she was guiding him per Duke Morecap's wishes and that Kahlen was a pawn. A beautiful, strong, and pleasurable pawn. A pawn she knew she loved and wanted. A pawn that must be ready for some great deed. A pawn she would give her mind, body, and soul to and then never see again. Ivy forced a smile and told Kahlen "on the bright side, all we have to do is survive until it is safe to travel the Gold Sea". Kahlen asked Ivy how certain she was that they would survive given that there was no chance to heal the land, and Ivy shrugged her shoulders and said, "I'm not certain. But I am convinced that I would only face this with you at my side." Kahlen brightened at Ivy's words and kissed her softly on her forehead and then more firmly on her lips. Ivy opened her mouth slightly and darted her tongue in and out of Kahlen's mouth. Ivy kissed Kahlen back and dragged her nails down his back and he moaned and twitched. Ivy raised her eyebrow and joked "let's practice how we will get through those cold nights, boy," and pushed Kahlen to the ground in a practiced manner.

The morning came and went, and Ivy and Kahlen were now out of the Basin and into a land that looked alien to them. Little to no vegetation and the brownish-gray soil hard and unforgiving on their feet made this place seem more of a wasteland than even The Orphans did. Ivy told Kahlen that she could smell the salty air of the sea although neither could see or hear it. Ivy reasoned that they were at least two days from the ocean and another week or more after that from the Fortress by the Sea. Ivy surmised that the salt in the air must have poisoned the ground so that nothing could grow, but even as she finished the thought she doubted her own reasoning. They were miles from the sea and yet less than a mile behind them laid the most fertile soil in the world. Ivy then reversed from her initial deduction and said

"Magic." Kahlen said "what about magic?" and rested his hands on Ivy's hips and kissed the nape of her neck. Ivy rocked back and forth and answered, "It takes a mystic, a healer according to legend to commune with the land and put it at rest." Kahlen continued his line of questioning. "How did they do it? What kind of mystic also can heal?" Ivy let Kahlen's question settle in her mind and then said, "I don't really know. I've never met anyone who could just heal a person let alone an entire land." Kahlen's interest was now piqued and he asked, "So, what if it is all a story? What if the land has always been this way and it can't be healed? What then?"

Ivy found the accusations disquieting, but she knew that at the core they rang true. There must be some other explanation to the history. Ivy knew for certain that the Fortress by the Sea had been manned by her people for over four hundred years, and that the tradition held that a mystic and a protector would always call the castle home until the next generation was ready. She couldn't place her finger on the answer as it stayed just out of reach much like she would when she played tag with her friends as a child. They had days to ponder such questions so she let it rest for the moment.

Two blissfully uneventful days, well, uneventful aside from passionate, impromptu lovemaking sessions, passed when the sea crested over the horizon for the first time. To Kahlen, this was the first time he felt normal, like he was home, since his adventure first began. Ivy had seen the sea before, but the smells and tastes were foreign to her and for the first time she was uncomfortable in her surroundings. Ivy dared not approach the surf as it roiled and crashed sending spray into the air, where it hung for a moment before showering them with a fine mist. Kahlen inhaled deeply and said, "C'mon Ivy, let's go for a swim," and before Ivy could protest, Kahlen stripped and thundered into the foam of an incoming wave. Ivy held her breath as Kahlen went under for what seemed an eternity and did not dare breathe until he bobbed up and waved for her to join him. Ivy put on a brave face and peeled off her clothes slowly with a hope that Kahlen would tire of the water and come back out. Ivy removed the last of her clothes and made her way to the water. Kahlen could see that she was scared to come in and he swam back to the beach and strode out of the water with his hand outstretched. Ivy's mouth curled up into a wicked little smile at the sight of her man. Ivy's eyes feasted upon Kahlen's so very naked body rising from the waves like a merman minus the fish tail. Kahlen reached Ivy and he told her that wading in "makes it worse. Better to just dive in and get used to the water all at once." Ivy nodded and held Kahlen's hand and they dove together. Ivy let Kahlen guide her through the water and they splashed around like children. The sea let them know it was time to get out as the swells grew in strength and in number.

Kahlen and Ivy dressed and made their way down the beach, tired from the swim but invigorated by the playfulness of the moment. They walked together, often hand in hand, and found that a simple look sometimes spoke volumes more than their words. Ivy asked Kahlen if it was "okay to go hunt?" Kahlen knew this meant that Ivy needed to change into her bear form and he obliged happily. Even though Ivy could change at will, she loved that Kahlen accepted her, all of her, and she derived pleasure from asking him for permission. She also loved that Kahlen repeatedly told her that she didn't need to ask. She enjoyed a level of trust with Kahlen that she quite frankly didn't know could exist, and was as free now to be who she was—as if she was alone in the woods. Ivy would never want to be alone again yet she knew that someday soon, she would be.

When the big bear rumbled up the beach, Kahlen waited with open arms and embraced her. He paid special attention to just behind Ivy's ears, where if he scratched just the right way would lead her to rolling onto her back in a submissive pose. Kahlen joked that he was probably the only man who had "a woman and a pet all rolled into one". Ivy changed to her human form and cursed Kahlen, while she chased him in circles until Kahlen surrendered. They made love on the beach and then camped for the night. Ivy caught a pair of huge pinkish gray fish loaded with fat that made for a tasty meal. The next day they took the leftovers they had dried and stuffed the carry pack till it overflowed. Ivy estimated that they had enough food for at least another three days, but only enough water for one. They would have to go further inland and find water—and they needed to do it fast. Kahlen doused the fire and they turned south to search for fresh water.

Kahlen and Ivy traveled for half a day and all they saw was mile after mile of cracked earth. They had conserved their water but faced a difficult choice. They could try and make it to The Orphans where fresh water would be likely or they could try for the Fortress by the Sea and hope they came across fresh water along the way. Regardless, they guessed they were two full days from either location with little more than half a day's worth of fresh water. While they debated which direction to head, Kahlen and Ivy sat back to back munching on the dried fish. After eating, they both took brief sips of water and that's when Kahlen took a chance when he decided, "I think we head to the Fortress, Ivy. I think that we are as likely to die out here no matter where we go. I think that you have led me here for a reason and I believe in you." Ivy was not as sure as Kahlen, but he sounded as if he spoke the truth. Ivy closed her eyes and said, "I will follow you. I will not leave your side." Kahlen sprung to his feet with a purpose and leaned down and helped Ivy to her feet. It was growing dark and she was tired, but Kahlen assured her that they would be better off going now and taking advantage of the cooler evening in order to save the water. Kahlen tapped his staff and light flooded the path ahead of them.

Kahlen reckoned that they had walked for nearly eight hours as the sun crept up behind them. There was enough daylight now for Kahlen to stop using his staff. Ivy slowed her pace and began to yawn which, in turn caused Kahlen to yawn. They had made great time overnight and were just hours from the sea. Kahlen wanted to keep going but Ivy asked to stop "for just a little while", so they sat and snacked on fish and sipped their water. A chilly breeze arose and Kahlen wished that there was something here to burn. There was neither scrub nor any driftwood to be seen. Kahlen jogged in a circle some one hundred and fifty feet from where Ivy sat, her eye lids deadened to the point where she could no longer keep them open. Kahlen could not find anything to burn and the chill worsened to the point where he suddenly saw his breath in the air. Kahlen began to shiver and he vigorously rubbed his hands together to fight the cold. He rushed back to Ivy and he tried to wake her. He wanted her to turn into bear form so that she could be warm and maybe he could huddle beside her and reduce his exposure. Ivy did not respond and Kahlen could not get her to stir. So exhausted, Kahlen wondered if Ivy could even turn if she did wake up.

Something new happened as the wind whipped up into a full gale, chilling Kahlen to the bone, and he hugged Ivy close to his chest and she was ice cold. Kahlen felt the wet, sloppy flakes of snow smack him in the face and panic set in. They were alone, completely exposed without shelter, and now a freak storm was trying to bury them alive. Snow began to pile up quickly all around them and it caked their hair and clung to their clothes like a frigid blanket. Kahlen tried to fend off the cold with his staff but the fire light did little more than melt the snow. Undeterred, Kahlen melted more snow and he collected as much of it as he could in their water pouches. He put the water pouches back into his carry pack and slipped. He changed the fire light to pure light and looked where he slipped. It wasn't ice. It was smooth and hard just like glass. It was only in a small area, but Kahlen wondered, and so he concentrated on the ground and the staff erupted in fire, scorching the ground leaving it like glass. Kahlen picked up the glass and it was solid. He jammed it into the ground and dragged Ivy to it. The glass acted as a buffer and it was warm to the touch. Kahlen, his face a mask of fury and determination, scorched wider patches of the ground and heaved the heavy pieces up from the ground and jammed them all around the prone Ivy. He created enough glass to surround them both and then he blasted a very wide area and dragged it back to Ivy. Kahlen hauled the glass up on its edge and propped it on top of the makeshift glass wall he had erected to protect Ivy. Kahlen grabbed the sheet of glass firmly with both hands, ignored the fact that his hands were being cut deeply and with a ferocious yell, pulled the huge sheet over their heads completely blocking the snow and wind. Kahlen urged his staff to evenly disperse a low heat within this glass tomb and he had a flashback to when he fell into the ancient shrine and found this staff with the body in the glass coffin.

Kahlen brought one of the freshly filled water pouches to Ivy's lips and begged her to drink. He dabbed the water on her lips and then tried to pour the water into her mouth but spilled the majority of it. Desperate, Kahlen took a small mouthful of water and brought his lips to hers and slowly let the water drip from his mouth into hers. Ivy opened her mouth just enough to take more water in and opened her eyes. Kahlen held her so tightly that Ivy could barely breathe. Ivy complained about being tired and thirsty so Kahlen told her to drink as much as she could. Ivy tried to sit up and struck her head on the glass roof. Kahlen apologized and did his best to explain what happened, and Ivy stared at him with wonder. Ivy croaked "you're telling me that you built a glass house for us?" She hugged Kahlen's arm. One spot where the roof did not rest evenly on the glass support pieces allowed the snow that melted when it struck the roof to drip directly into a water pouch. Kahlen watched the snow pile up around them but the warmth within the shelter kept the roof clear. Ivy sipped some more water and then curled into Kahlen's waiting arms and fell back to sleep. Kahlen hugged Ivy to his chest and he drifted off to sleep.

Kahlen woke to a soft, loving kiss from Ivy who declared "you are my hero. I love you." Kahlen answered with an "I love you, too" before she finished her sentiment. Ivy then said, "Now, how do we get out of here?" with a laugh. Kahlen guessed that at least three feet of snow surrounded them and even with his staff he did not know how they could safely venture to the Fortress. Ivy ran her fingers over the glass roof and complimented Kahlen for his craftsmanship as this was as smooth and clear as any glass she had ever seen. Ivy punched it hard and it didn't move or crack. At closer inspection, Kahlen noticed that there was a slight curve to the glass that reminded him of the bow of a ship. It also looked like the hauling sled Dock Master Averill used in Crescent Bay. "I've got it!" Kahlen exclaimed. "Got what?" answered Ivy. "A sled. This can be a sled. That's how we go forward. I will pull you and our supplies over the snow and we can get through this and find the Fortress," an overly excited Kahlen belched out. Kahlen, with Ivy's help, slid the roof from their shelter and it rested on top of the snow bank. Kahlen then sent a piercing ray of light through the glass and made two large holes. Kahlen rummaged through their packs and found two tattered shirts and about seven feet of rope that he secured to the holes in the glass sheet creating a huge loop. He stepped inside the loop and leaned into the fabric and when he stepped the glass sheet slid smoothly over the snow. Kahlen, proud of his ingenuity told Ivy to sit on the sled, and he started to remove the two carry packs from his back and placed them on the sled. Ivy never moved and instead said "you saved me last night. Now, it's my turn." Ivy yanked her clothes off and threw them to Kahlen, pointed to the pack and as soon as her clothes were packed away turned into the great bear. As a bear, Ivy frolicked in the snow and quickly nuzzled Kahlen and pushed him back onto the sled. Ivy tucked her head inside of the loop and put the rope in her mouth. Ivy pulled the sled and when she was sure that Kahlen was going to be safe broke into a full run. For the better part of the night, Kahlen forgot that they faced almost certain death and let the joy of the moment carry him as much as the sled itself did.

Ivy grew tired in the early morning hours and changed back to her female form and immediately regretted it as the cold nearly froze her in place. Kahlen helped her dress and this time he was able to show Ivy how he made the shelter last night. They worked together and soon were warm inside the shelter. A little safe haven in the middle of a brutal storm, but it was home for a night and they were thankful to face the elements together.

They did not sleep as long as the previous day and had plenty of daylight to guide them. Tired, but excited for what was to come, Ivy transformed and pulled Kahlen once again. Less than three hours later Ivy changed form and she jumped into Kahlen's arms and kissed him over and over. Kahlen gave back as many kisses as he received and asked, "What was that for?" Ivy just pointed, and there it was. A huge silhouette on a lone bluff, a monument to ancient craftsmen, the Fortress by the Sea. Ivy changed once more and she clambered over and through snow banks until they reach the front gate. The door was pieced together with various woods and Kahlen was sure that he recognized bow planks among the wood. Kahlen and Ivy pushed until the door moved enough for them to squeeze through. A massive courtyard filled with snow greeted them, and so they pushed on until they reached the ornate doors that led to the main keep. Kahlen looked at Ivy and she nodded her approval, and Kahlen heaved into the doors expecting resistance.

Ivy was still laughing at Kahlen and pantomimed his pratfall. The massive doors moved far more easily than Kahlen expected, and when he drove his shoulder into them he was caught off guard when they opened so quickly sending him sprawling onto the floor face first. Although cold, the interior of the main hall was inviting and there were signs of the last guardians sent here. Art, clothing, and even handmade furniture that Ivy had last seen four years ago at the underground market beneath her home. Weapons were mounted on hooks all throughout the Fortress including native blades and shiny black maces and clubs.

A massive stack of wood sat beside an empty hearth, so Kahlen went to work on starting a fire while Ivy searched the adjoining rooms on the main floor to see what she could find. The majority of the rooms were bedrooms and Ivy found several blankets as well as two or three outfits made for women. In the largest bedroom there was a cradle and more clothes, including five or six tiny outfits fit for a baby. In a cedar chest, Ivy found two long fur coats and two oversized dresses made from a very light, gauzy fabric. Ivy smiled at Kahlen as she moved from room to room. On the far side of the room Ivy found the hallway that led to a large kitchen and an empty storeroom. Ivy could smell the fire from the main room and she could feel the temperature change as the air warmed. Ivy climbed a nearby staircase and went to the second floor. The majority of the rooms were empty save two. One room was wall to wall with books and parchments and artifacts. The second room had a beautiful desk and beside the desk was a painting of a one legged man, and a beautiful woman holding a sleeping baby. Ivy brought the painting downstairs and asked Kahlen to mount it above the hearth. Kahlen asked Ivy "are these the people from your story?" Ivy said pride fully "yes. The very first guardians sent here."

Further inspection turned up a man's heavy long coat but no clothes that could properly fit Kahlen. Kahlen did find an old trap door that led below the main hall, into a root cellar and much to his delight, to a freshwater stream. Kahlen used his staff to illuminate the cellar and a number of buckets and nets were carefully stacked on carved wood shelves. Kahlen stripped then waded into the stream and was surprised to see fish, large fish at that, swimming against the current and heading south away from the sea. It was cold and the current stronger than he expected, and Kahlen guessed that the stream fed into the ocean but did not recall seeing an outlet on the surface, so he questioned whether or not it simply returned to the ground. Kahlen explored the stream as far north as he could. The stream was at least six or seven feet deep but the earthen ceiling closed to the water's surface. Satisfied he could move no further, Kahlen worked his way upstream, a more challenging feat than he expected and rested when he reached the stairs that led back to the trap door. After a minute's rest, Kahlen splashed back into the stream and this time he brought his staff. Eight, maybe nine steps upstream later, Kahlen stepped and found no footing. Kahlen had to swim in place and the current appeared to strengthen. Kahlen blasted light as far into the water as it would go and he could see no bottom. He took a deep breath and then drove down. Kahlen swam for fifteen seconds and the light barely allowed him to see three feet in any direction. Kahlen blew air out of his lungs once he crested the surface of the water and allowed the current to propel him toward the cellar steps.

Kahlen sat on the stream's bank and a small flash of light caught his eye on the wall opposite of where he sat. He jumped back into the stream and in three steps found the object. It was a polished hook, made from a smooth, black metal and it suddenly became obvious. Kahlen launched himself from that side of the stream and landed safely upon the other. He went through the piled netting and found one that had loops on strings on the top corners. Kahlen searched the area near the steps until his staff reflected off of another black metal hook. He secured one end of the net to each hook and watched two fish smack right into it. Kahlen grabbed a bucket with his left hand and scooped up one fish and then just used his right hand to grab the other, and he plopped it into the bucket. Kahlen put the bucket onto the ground and then grabbed the bottom of the net and flipped it over the top, leaving plenty of room for the fish to swim freely until he needed to catch more.

Ivy was startled when Kahlen's head popped up from beneath the floor. Ivy laughed nervously and then smirked when she said, "Leave it to you to go into a dungeon and come back with fresh fish." Kahlen described their good fortune and after handing Ivy the fish descended into the cellar once more and retrieved two buckets of water. Ivy and Kahlen ate well and fell asleep in each other's arms by the fire.

Sometime during the night, a storm began to rage and even the hearth could not keep the hall warm. Ivy woke first and shook Kahlen awake. Kahlen flashed light and was surprised to see his breath hang in the air. Kahlen tossed several logs onto the fire and used his staff to light them, which helped a little but they needed to almost crawl into the fire to avoid the cold. "We have to stay off of the floor and conserve heat," Kahlen said. Ivy and Kahlen ran to the nearest bedroom and hauled a bed into the main hall. Then they rushed to find as much clothing and bedding they could find. Bundled in layer after layer and huddled as close to the fire as they dared, Kahlen and Ivy hugged each other on top of the bed.

After a short time, Ivy and Kahlen had started to feel like they were going to survive the cold. They stopped shivering and their teeth stopped chattering. Ivy even made some jokes about this being a trick to get her into bed and so on. Just above their heads was the painting of the first guardians. Kahlen remarked at how happy they looked. Ivy remarked at how warm they looked. Kahlen thought about that for a moment and said "look at all the grasses in the background. It looks like the Basin but that painting was done from atop this castle. See, in the bottom left corner is part of the main gate. This was a fine place to have a family." Ivy pondered Kahlen's words and made the comment, "I wonder if that's how they found the land or if that's how the land was after they healed it?" Kahlen hugged Ivy close to his chest and shrugged his shoulders. Kahlen was about to say something else when the fire was snuffed out, chilling the hall so quickly that frost could be seen creeping across the floor. Kahlen lashed out at the hearth with his staff but his flame light did not stir life into the logs. In fact, the more he tried to light a fire the colder the hall became. The frost crept closer and started to climb one leg of their bed. Kahlen urged Ivy to run for the back stairs and they moved as quickly as they could and just beat the ice to the stairs. They climbed the stairs and went to the bedroom where Ivy had found the painting. Kahlen pushed the desk in front of the door after they closed the door behind them. Ivy jumped upon the bed and Kahlen tried unsuccessfully to start a fire. Kahlen cursed the staff repeatedly and then he heard the door start to crack as a trickle of frost snaked under the door and the desk. They were trapped, and Ivy started to cry out "I'm so sorry. I brought you here. It's all my fault. I should never have agr..." her admission of guilt was interrupted by the most heartfelt and pure kiss she had ever known. Kahlen stood before Ivy and proclaimed his love and he said that "they could either let their end tell the tale of two people who couldn't fight off the cold and died in a pathetic heap, or a tale of two lovers who chose to face the end in a final embrace." Kahlen pulled layer after layer off of his body and stood defiantly before the encroaching ice. Ivy's blood burned with desire and she stood on the bed and threw her clothes at the floor and cursed the cold. Ivy lunged from the bed and Kahlen caught her from the air and pulled her onto him as he stood there. Ivy sighed and moaned as she wrapped her legs around Kahlen's waist until her feet touched. Ivy's moan grew louder once Kahlen entered her and she did not stop until they both erupted and collapsed upon the bed. They kissed softly and exclaimed their love for one another and never uncoupled, even when Ivy turned her body slowly until she faced away from Kahlen and begged him to prove his love for her by making sure the whole world could hear her them. Kahlen wrapped Ivy's hair around his left fist and pulled back gently and whispered into her ear "the Gods will hear us" and he spent his last few minutes of life giving Ivy exactly what she wanted.

Birds chirped outside of the bedroom window. Ivy thought that when she joined her ancestors that she would be in the sky, not left to walk the earthly plane. At least the sun was out and as she peered out of the window she saw grass lead all the way to the beach. Ivy lamented the fact that she never had a chance to see this land, in this way, when she lived. Ivy was surprised when she felt the cool stone floor on her feet when she got out of bed. She was even more surprised when she smelled food. She knew that she smelled fish. Ivy was confused. She didn't know of any spirit that could smell food and when her stomach growled, would want to eat food. Ivy heard a clash of pans and hurried downstairs. To her surprise, the hearth held a small fire but the room was very comfortable even without clothes. Ivy heard Kahlen's voice. "Was he singing?" she thought and leaned around the corner and peeked into the kitchen. Kahlen, stood before the main oven and turned around with a smile and said "oh, good. You're up". Kahlen ran to Ivy and kissed her hard on the lips and then more playfully over the rest of her face. Ivy asked seriously "are you a spirit too?" to which Kahlen only shook his head. Ivy asked "what happened?" and Kahlen told her that when they collapsed together last night for the last time that they threw the covers off of the bed and just held each other and kissed. He added that they both agreed to hold each other and to not close their eyes until the cold took them. Kahlen laughed and said "we healed the land." Ivy asked "how could that be? We have tasted each other many times. Why would last night heal the land but none of the other times do so?" Kahlen didn't know and he didn't care, and he picked up Ivy effortlessly and kissed her once more and told her "breakfast is almost ready. I hope you are hungry." He went back to the oven. Ivy was indeed hungry. They ate at the dining table at the back of the kitchen and Ivy finished her share and most of Kahlen's, who laughed and said, "It's a good thing I've got another fish in the oven," and "you know I did an awful lot of the work last night. I deserve a little bit." Ivy stared at Kahlen and knew she adored him. He was beautiful and tough. He was smart and fierce. He was hers and she never thought she could feel so loved. Ivy sniffed as tears wet her cheek. Ivy was a little embarrassed by her emotional release and Kahlen asked her if everything was alright. Ivy smiled through the tears and assured him that she had never been happier. Truth be told, Kahlen was not so sure what was going on with Ivy, but she did smile at him with a warmth and kindness that comforted him. Ivy promised Kahlen that these were "tears of joy" and that she was just so thankful to be alive, with him, right here in this place that she couldn't hold it all in.

Kahlen accepted Ivy's explanation without another question and he told her how the courtyard was green and that he could've sworn that there were fruits and vegetable growing in rows. Kahlen told Ivy all about the small herd of cows that were grazing just outside of the main gate. Ivy sniffed the air and concentrated on the smells that wafted in and around the hall. She said that there were berries and herbs growing nearby and that she would show him how to identify them and harvest them. Ivy admitted that she did not know how they healed the land but she was sure that they had done just that. She strolled into the main hall and stopped in front of the hearth and smiled at the painting. The stories were all true. Guardians did come here and apparently still did.

She silently thanked the happy family staring back at her from the painting and her eyes passed from the man to the woman and finally to the child. Ivy found herself absorbed with the painting and it was then she first noticed that the sun in the painting appeared to shine more intensely on the child. So intensely that the child had a subtle glow and at the child's feet the grass was more vibrant and the flowers in full bloom. Ivy shook her head and said "no...Could it? Am I? Are we?" and held her hand to her belly. Ivy sucked her bottom lip under her top teeth and glanced side to side, and then locked eyes with the woman in the painting. Ivy knew how she and Kahlen had healed the land, and she could not wait to tell Kahlen all about it.

EPILOGUE

Ivy planned on surprising Kahlen with the news that she was carrying his child. She wanted the moment to be perfect. Ideas of how and where and when danced in and out her mind and yet she could not think of the perfect way. She felt subtle changes to her body and her senses were sharper than ever. She felt a power surge deep within and a sense of purpose and pride she could barely contain. She had snuck away to clean the linens that were designed for the ornate cradle on the second floor and had dried them among lilacs a few hundred yards from the fort. Every day that passed was another lost opportunity to surprise Kahlen, so Ivy made a silent declaration that she would simply tell Kahlen while they ate dinner this evening.

Ivy looked up at the sun and basked in its warmth. She twirled around and laughed like a child until she was dizzy. Ivy plopped to the grass, cool at the roots but soft and warm where the sun brushed it. Ivy lay in the grass until her head stopped spinning and the leaned upon one elbow facing the sea. She pressed her hand against her belly, not yet swollen and thought of names. Certain it was a girl, Ivy focused on names native to her home with an occasional nod to names popular south of the Orphans.

Ivy had lost track of time and saw how far to the west the sun had traveled. There was no doubt about it. She would tell Kahlen tonight and as she stepped through the grass toward the fort she smelled an acrid scent clinging to the gentle breeze coming off of the sea. The nearer the fort the stronger the scent grew. Far above, Kahlen stood atop the highest wall, his body facing the sea and the moment Ivy crested the small hill on the western side of the fort she could see what Kahlen was staring at.

Three boats worked feverishly to reach the old dock north of the fort. Ivy trained her eyes on the lead boat and concentrated until she could make out a specter standing tall in the bow. It was Duke Morecap. Ivy felt the weight of the world collapse upon her and turned her look upward where Kahlen met her eyes. Kahlen raced down to the courtyard, out through the main gate and rushed to Ivy's side. Kahlen saw the sadness and fear in Ivy's eyes and pulled her in close whispering his love for her. Even Kahlen could hear the men in the ships, and he told Ivy to go back into the fort and prepare to run. Ivy told Kahlen "they are not here do us harm" and then "they are here to take us to your destiny".

Kahlen wore his confusion like a mask as Ivy walked away from him and headed to the tall man striding over the sand in their direction. Kahlen walked as if in a fog, following Ivy to the beach where Duke Morecap met them with a hearty "Hello". Kahlen did not return the greeting and it was not until he heard the man call Ivy by name followed by, "I see your journey has left you well". The Duke turned from Ivy with a pat upon her shoulder and told her "well done".

The Duke turned his attention to Kahlen and told him "you will need to be a good host but only for two nights and then you, Kahlen Bowsprit, Knight of Crescent Bay, will save the world".